# *Just* Make Him *Beautiful*

A NOVEL BY MIKE W.

# Just Make Him Beautiful

## MIKE WARREN

Life Changing Books in conjunction with Power Play Media
Published by Life Changing Books
P.O. Box 423 Brandywine, MD 20613

Library of Congress Cataloging-in-Publication Data;

www.lifechangingbooks.net
13 Digit: 978-1934230657
10 Digit: 1-934230650

Follow us on Twitter: www.twitter.com/lcbooks

# Dedication

I would like to dedicate this fourth novel of mine to the loved ones that I lost this past year.

In loving memory of my younger brother:
Anthony D. Hill Sr.
And in loving memory of my daughter:
Lakeshia D. Hill

I truly love and miss you both.

# Acknowledgements

I first want to thank my family for their love and support of my work and their understanding.

Secondly, my partner, Anthony L. Parker who is my biggest fan and supporter.

To all of my fans who have encouraged me to continue my writing. I want to say thank you, you guys have no idea how much I appreciate the calls and the messages of support and love you guys send me everyday. It gives me the strength to continue.

I also want to thank Carlton Smith, Co-Founder & Vice President of Black Gay Pride Inc. and Kevin Clemons, Founder & Chair of Baltimore Black Pride Inc., who have supported my work since my first novel, "A Private Affair". You guys are "Awesome".

To all the book clubs, book stores and radio shows, thank you thank you thank you for your continue support.

Last but not least, I want to thank my Publisher Tressa Smallwood and all the LCB writers, let's do the dayum thing!

*Mike Warren*

becool031@yahoo.com
mhill3131@yahoo.com
www.facebook.com/mikewarren
www.mikewarren.yolasite.com
www.lifechangingbooks.com

# Chapter 1

"Sean, please go away! I don't want you to see me like this," I screamed, trying to hide myself against the wall.

"What the fuck you doing?"Sean looked at me as though I was a ghost. "What's this shit about, Cam?"

My dragon sista girl, Akasha Casidene, came to my defense. "Ah, excuse me, honey," she said. "I don't know who you are, but you need to leave my sista girl alone. Now, just because I'm in this dress and heels don't mean I can't throw down. Don't get it twisted."

Sean got in her face. "Look, bitch, you betta step off before I fuck you up."

This is really not what I had expected to go down. I mean, I still loved Sean with all my heart, and I just wanted to surprise him with a little song and dance, so the last thing I wanted was for a fight to break out.

Just as I was about to get between Akasha and Sean, the club's security showed up. "Yo, my brotha, come on, man. Let's chill this out. What's the problem here?"

While security pulled Sean aside, I grabbed Akasha's arm, and we both got back into the limo.

"*Giiiiiirl*, I don't know what his problem is. Who was he?" Akasha pulled out her compact and checked her makeup.

"That was Sean," I replied, feeling sad.

"Ooh, chile. Not the one and only Mr. Sean Mathews?"

"The one and only." My eyes were beginning to well up.

"My! You said he was fine, and you didn't lie either, girl. Hell, the only reason I didn't kick him in the nuts or his dick was because I thought I might get a chance to taste them later. *Kee-kee-kee-kee!*"

"Chile, boo," I replied, waving my hand at her and wiping my eyes with the other.

"But, seriously, do you still wanna do this?"

"I think so," I answered, not sure of what I really wanted to do.

"Driver, can you just go around to the back entrance please."

"Yes, ma'am, not a problem."

Within seconds, we were at the back door entrance. Unfortunately, the door was locked, so my girl Akasha began banging on the door like she was the police.

A security guard held the door open for us to enter. "Ms. Akasha, why are you out here banging on the back door?"

"Thanks, Al, but you don't even wanna know. Oh, this is my girl, Camira Saxton. Tonight will be her first time performing."

"*Dayum*, Camira! You fine as shit, girl.Come on over here and give daddy some love."

"Al, don't try it. You keep on and I'ma tell yo' wife on you."

Akasha grabbed my hand and led me downstairs to what I assumed was the dressing rooms. And, Lawd knows, not a moment too soon, because Al was a big ol', burly, greasy-looking brotha, and I knew he just wanted to cop a feel.

"Girl, you got your music?" Akasha asked as we entered the small dressing room.

"Yeah, it's in my bag. Why?"

"Give it to me so I can take it to the DJ to queue it up."

"I'm not ready now. I don't go on for another hour or so."

"I swear, you new dragons kill me."

"What?"

"Ms. Camira Saxton, the DJ needs to have your music queued so that when you do go on stage, your music will be ready. I bet you probably thought you wouldn't give it to him until you were about to go on stage, huh?"

"No," I snapped, not really understanding what difference it made.

I handed Akasha my music to give to the DJ and began unpacking the outfit I brought to perform in. I'd been rehearsing Beyonce's "Single Ladies" for the past couple of weeks, just for Mr. Sean Mathews. As my sista girl Akasha was helping me with my transformation into the "drag queen world," we both realized just how much I looked like Beyoncé, so hence the choice of song. But, not to toot my own horn, I looked so much better. Besides, the only thing Ms. Beyoncé had over me was her coins, okay!

I sat in front of the lighted mirror and stared at my reflection. *How did I get to this point in my life?*

"Hey, ma. How you doing?" this gorgeous, young, dark-skinned brother asked.

"Ah, hello," I replied, somewhat startled.

"My bad. I didn't mean to scare you, ma." He held his hand out to shake mine.

"Oh, dear chile, no, no, no. It would take a lil more man than you to scare a lady like me," I replied as I held my hand out, letting him know he may kiss it, as a gentleman should.

"My name is Mike, and you are, beautiful?" he asked as he leaned down to kiss the back of my hand.

"Camira Saxton," I replied, staring at him, wondering where I'd seen him before.

Just then this short Puerto Rican dude interrupted our conversation. "Yo, Mike, I just seen Sean come in the club. Can

**3**

you help me get ready?"

"A'ight, man, I'll be right there," Mike told him. Then he turned to me and said, "Well, Camira, it was a pleasure meeting you."

"Of course, it was. I see Sean still likes things done his way and in a timely manner, huh?" I asked with a hint of sarcasm.

"Oh, so you know Sean?" Mike asked.

"Biblically," I answered with a smile.

Mike looked at me as though he didn't understand my response. Then he walked away. And even though he didn't know who I was, I knew he must have been one of Sean's boys. Which caused me to wonder, *Why didn't Sean ever pick me to be one of his boys? Hmmm?*

As I sat there looking in the mirror and reapplying my makeup, I heard all this yelling going on upstairs. I couldn't make out the voices, so I continued to apply my makeup.

Next thing I know, Akasha came down the steps cussing and bitching up a storm. "Girl, who got your wig in a knot?" I asked.

"You won't believe who's here," she huffed.

"Who?" I asked, not really caring one way or the other.

"That 'draga-surous' Ms. Bi-bi Lemoore. That bitch!"

"Who's that?" I asked, puzzled.

"You remember the bitch that wanted to fight me down at Club Bunnz about a month or so ago because she claimed I stole her tired-ass lip-gloss?"

"Oh, yeah, I remember now. What is she doing here?"

"She gonna get her ass killed, she keep fuckin' with me," Akasha yelled.

At that moment, I heard footsteps coming down the stairs. I knew some shit was about to jump off.

Ms. Lemoore approached Akasha with fire in her eyes. "Bitch, you gonna do what?"

"I said you gonna…"

Before Akasha had a chance to finish her sentence, Ms.

4

Lemoore swung and punched my girl right in the jaw. Akasha lost her balance, and her ass fell dead on the floor. I felt kinda bad for Akasha because there were other performers standing around laughing and kee-keeing.

Ms. Lemoore looked at me. "And what you gonna do, *biotch*?" she sneered at me with her hands on her hips, her head moving from side to side.

The last thing I wanted to do was get into it with this six-foot, hoochie-thug drag queen that looked like an alien with heels on, but what choice did I have? And even though I considered myself to be a lady, I jumped up from my seat with my hands balled and yelled, "I know you're not talking to me, you E.T.-looking bitch!"

Well, thank God for Mike because Ms. Lemoore charged towards me, and all I could see was the steam rising up from her two-dollar wig as she balled up her fist.

Just before my legs were about to buckle, Mike grabbed her from behind and shoved her against the wall and calmly stated to her, "I don't think you wanna do that to Ms. Camira now, do you?"

She yelled, "Get the fuck off me, you faggot!"

At that point, Ms. Ineedaman and security came running downstairs to see what all the commotion was about. Once it was explained, security escorted Ms. Lemoore out of the building.

"Look, y'all, we are already running late. The show should have started thirty minutes ago. Now can we start the show, please?" Ms. Ineedaman pleaded.

As the performers began to spread out and prepare for their routine, I went over and kneeled in front of Akasha to make sure she was okay. "Akasha, wake up," I said, slapping her in the face.

"I'm here, I'm here," she replied, coming to.

"Good. It's showtime. Let's get ready." I helped her to her feet.

"You know that bitch just got a lucky punch," Akasha

stated as she stumbled to her feet. "But you wait until I see her ass again."

I know Akasha was only saying that to save face, but the truth is, Ms. Lemoore knocked her the fuck out, and she would have done the same to me if it weren't for Mike. I definitely had to thank him for coming to my rescue.

Akasha went into the restroom to freshen herself up, and I took my seat at the mirror and thought about how fine Mike really was. *Hmmm, my knight in shining armor*, I thought to myself.

"You a'ight, Ms. Camira?" Mike touched me on my shoulder.

"Oh, Mike, you startled me," I said, looking up at him.

He smiled. "I thought you said it would take a li'l bit more of a man than me to scare you?"

"I didn't say you scared me. I said you startled me. There is a difference, sweetheart," I snapped, trying not to look at him too hard.

"Dayum! My bad, ma. And why you so mean anyway? You ain't got a man or sumf'n?" Mike asked in his sexy, thugged-out voice.

"Why you so concern?" I thought about what I was about to say and realized that Mike didn't deserve my diva attitude. After all, he'd just come to my rescue, and while he stood there with these jean shorts on and his manhood swinging all over the place, causing my hormones to go into overdrive, I needed to chill.

I took a deep breath. "Look, Mike, I apologize for my attitude, and thank you for taking care of that six-foot alien." I smiled.

"Aw! There you go. See, you're really pretty when you smile."

"So, what you're saying is I'm not pretty if I don't smile?"

"Naw, Ms. Camira. I think you're very attractive," he replied, stooping down and looking at me at eye level.

"Li'l boy, what are you tryin'-a do?"

"Li'l boy, Ms. Camira? You ain't that much older than me. And what do you think I'm doing?" he asked, rubbing his hand up and down my leg.

"Correct me if I'm wrong, but don't you have to ask Sean for his consent to try to get in someone else's pants?" I batted my eyes.

"Something like that, but I'm sure he wouldn't have a problem with you."

"You think so, huh? Wow. You have no idea as to who I am, do you?"

"Ah, should I?" he asked, looking into my eyes as though he was trying to figure out who I was.

"Why don't you go ask Sean?"

"Okay, I will," he said, rising from the floor and walking away.

"Hey, where you going?"

"I'm going to ask Sean who you are. Now, don't go anywhere, gorgeous. I'll be right back." Mike smiled, climbing the steps two at a time.

*Chile, boo*, I thought to myself. *These kids today are a mess. And I know he couldn't be no older than twenty-two, if that, and tryin'-a get with someone like me. Humph! The nerve. However, I will admit, he's a big boy. Lawd have mercy. Young, chocolate, and fine. I do give Sean credit for having good taste.*

*

Hmmm, Sean Mathews. What can I say about Sean? For those of you who don't know, I, Camira Saxton aka Cameron Jenkins, happened to be the love of Sean Mathews' life.

I'd met Sean just about four years ago, right after I'd graduated from Basic Training and AIT (Advance Individual Training), which was when I'd first noticed him. Yeah, chile, can you imagine...me in Uncle Sam's Army?

Fort George G. Meade, Maryland was my first duty station, and Sean became my roommate. I had found out, through a good friend of mine who worked in the administration office on base that he was from Maryland, and that's where he was going to be stationed. Well, honies, that's all I needed to know.

Mr. Sean Mathews was what I always prayed for. Starting when I was a teen, every night I used to pray, please God, just make him beautiful. And that Sean was.

I pulled some strings, so to speak, and had my orders changed to Fort George G. Meade, Maryland as well.

*

Wow, I remember it just like it was yesterday. I had gotten there before Sean and decided which side of the room I wanted. I had unpacked my belongings, decorated the room with a white fur rug with matching comforter, and changed out of that tired army-green uniform. Then I put on my leopard Speedo and my fierce straw hat and stood in my full-length mirror singing my girl Patti Labelle's hit, "Lady Marmalade." Thinking back, I really thought I was the shit.

But when Sean entered the room, chile, he looked like a black Arnold Schwarzenegger. I couldn't wait to show him my skills.

Unfortunately, as time went on, I learned he was a married man with a family in Baltimore. Needless to say, this didn't discourage me. I'd dealt with several brothas who were married or had girlfriends. So for me, this only meant it would just take a little longer.

But, truth be told, it took almost two years before Sean and I actually did the wild thing. And can you believe it happened the night before I was to get married? Dayum straight, no pun intended. Right after the bachelor party he threw in my honor. After that, baby, his nose was wide open.

Sean and I had been through a lot, but if nothing else, we always maintained a close friendship. But since he won that "sir" contest and started initiating all these "boys," and relocated to Hawaii, our friendship had become strained.

Now, I knew deep down, he still loved me. Even though

he became angry when he first saw me outside, I knew that was only because he was caught off guard and didn't know I had transformed myself into this gorgeous creature.

*

Sitting here thinking of the good times Sean and I had shared, I began to hear the loud music and the audience yelling and screaming with laughter coming from upstairs as Ms. Ineedaman began introducing a few of the performers. Lucky for me, I wasn't going on until close to the end.

Oh, by the way, did I mention that Sean confessed his love for me on my wedding day? Chile, yes, he did. And trust me when I say, that was a big mess. In front of God, his family, my family, and our friends, he announced, "Cameron, I love you and want to be with you. Please don't make the same mistake I did."

Well, what was a girl to do? I mean, here I was, standing there with my not-too-bright bride, her father, the minister, and the guests staring at me, waiting for a response from li'l ol' me.

Just so you know, I've always been the type of girl who always wanted to be in a relationship. I've never been one of those hoes that wanted to be with a different man every night, like some of us gay men do. Don't get me wrong, I've done a lot of things in my past that I'm not proud of, and yes, I've had my share of one-night stands here and there, but it was with the hope that each of these men was the right one. But then I realized they were just saying whatever it took to get in my pants.

But when Sean Mathews came into my life, I knew God had answered my prayer.

I guess I should try to explain how I changed from being the little, skinny, curly-haired, country, naïve, light-skinned boy into this beautiful, sexy, exotic-looking female impersonator. Well, honies, don't clutch the pearls too tight. Sit back and let me tell you my story.

MIKE WARREN

# Chapter 2

## May 1997
## Fifteen years ago

"Aw, Cameron, I'ma tell Mommy on you," Keshia said.

"I don't care. Go ahead and tell Mommy. You just jealous 'cause you can't fit it."

"Fine," she said, stomping out of my room.

I don't know why my mother had to have another child. I was the baby up until six years ago, which was when my baby sister Keshia was born. Before then, it was my mom, my older brother Ray, and me.

My mom never got married. I guess, looking back on how things turned out, that's because she spent most of her time in a halfway house, but I'm getting ahead of myself.

Now eleven years old, I knew I was different since the tender age of four. When I started Pre-K, I found myself playing mostly with the little girls in my class instead of with the boys. I had no interest in playing with trucks, toy guns, or blocks. I preferred playing with baby dolls, combing their hair and dressing them up in different outfits. I was a li'l drag queen in the making.

When I had turned nine, I was called a sissy for the very first time. This stupid boy named Tyrone, who was in my class, got mad at me because our Math teacher, Mrs. Pender, asked him what the square root of 1,345 was and I raised my hand and got the answer right when he didn't know it. He got mad and called me a sissy out loud, and the rest of the kids in my class starting laughing. So, Ms. Pender sent him to the principal's office. I really didn't know how to feel, since I didn't know what the word *sissy* meant. Believe it or not, that was the first time I had ever heard the term.

When I got home, I asked my mother what it meant, and she informed me that that's what people call other boys who act like girls. I was devastated. I didn't know how I was ever going to be able to show my face in that school again.

*

The next day during lunchtime, Tyrone and his bullying ass came over to my table and asked me what time it was. At first, I didn't want to tell him because I didn't want him to see my new Mickey Mouse watch that Mother had just brought me for my birthday. As I tried to cover it with my hand, he suddenly grabbed my arm and snatched it off my wrist and walked away with it.

The other kids started to point and laugh at me. I was so hurt and embarrassed; I wanted to crawl into a hole.

For the rest of the day, I sat in class thinking, *How am I gonna get my watch back?* I couldn't tell Mother I'd just lost it. She would've never believed it because she knew how much I loved that watch and that I wasn't that irresponsible.

Honey, once that dreaded three o'clock school bell rang and kids began breaking their necks to get outside to go home, I thought that bully Tyrone would give it back. I walked up to him as he stood outside in the schoolyard with his friends.

"Can I have my watch back, please?" I asked in a squeaky tone, holding my trembling hand out.

"What? You want your watch back?" Tyrone questioned,

**12**

while he and his friends laughed hysterically.

"Yeah," I replied, softly and very pleadingly.

"Here. Here's your watch." And out of nowhere, Tyrone hauled off and punched me dead in my mouth. He hit me so hard, my little yella ass fell right on the ground. Then this muthafucka had the nerve to climb on top of me and began punching me like I stole something from him.

Chile, I started biting him everywhere I could. At one point, I think I bit him in the crotch, because he stopped punching me and bent over and grabbed himself. Honey, this was my chance to get the hell outta there.

I got my little yella ass up and started running as fast as I could. I looked behind me, and there was Tyrone and his friends not too far behind. Let me tell you, I was so scared and frightened, chile, I ran past my own house, twice. Darling, I know that shit might be funny now, but it wasn't at the time, because I had to keep running just to tire them fools out. Thank God, Mother never asked me about my watch.

\*

For the next couple of months, I used every excuse in the book not to go to school. I would play sick, or sometimes I would oversleep. My mom worked for the NTS (Nebraska Transit System) and she worked from three a.m. to twelve p.m. Monday through Saturday. As a single parent she volunteered for that schedule because of the night differential.

By the beginning of the third month, the school had sent a letter home via snail mail. My mother went off on me. "Cameron, bring your bony ass here," she yelled.

"Okay, Mother," I said, not knowing what I had done for her to sound so mad.

"Hurry up, boy," she continued to yell.

"Yes, ma'am," I replied as I stood in front of her.

She shook what appeared to be a letter all in my face. "What's the meaning of this?"

"I don't know," I replied timidly.

"This is a letter from your school letting me know that you've missed more than fifteen days this semester from school. Have your lost your everlasting mind?"

"No, ma'am," I said softly. I lowered my head down and looked at the floor.

"Now, I have to lose time from work and take you up to the school in the morning because they wanna meet with me. Take your skinny, high-yella ass to your room. I'll be there in a minute.

I began to cry as I ran to my room because when mother said, "Go to your room. I'll be there in a minute," that meant she was coming to beat that ass.

The worst part was the waiting. Sometimes she would make us wait for up to an hour or so. You see, I'm the type of person who wants to get it done and over with. I don't like having time to think about what I did wrong and think how bad that ass-whipping is going to be. I'm a do-it-and-get-it-over-with kinda girl.

Anywho, she wore my ass out that day, and I never played hooky ever again.

\*

When we were younger, my little sister and I used to play house. She was the daughter, and I was the mother. We lived in a two-bedroom apartment. My sister slept in Mother's room, and my big brother Ray and I shared a room. But since he was always out, hanging with his friends, I pretty much had the room to myself. That's why we would always play house in my room.

I didn't like having a baby sister because she thought that just because she was the only girl and the baby, she ought to get her way.

Mother didn't help the situation, because she always babied her. In essence, she was mommy's little girl.

Humph, if anything I could be more of a girl than her. Besides, I was older and already had a teenage girl's shape, even though I was only eleven.

**14**

"Cameron," Mother yelled as she stood in my bedroom doorway, jolting me from my thoughts.

I was so embarrassed as I stood there with one of her dresses on looking and admiring myself in the floor-length mirror.

"What are you doing?" Mother asked, sounding angry.

My baby sister, smiling and extending her tongue out at me, stood behind Mother.

"Nothing," I replied, not knowing what else to say.

"Why are you wearing my dress?" she asked in a disappointing tone.

I started to stutter, "I-I-I thought it was pretty. We were playing house, and Keshia got mad because she couldn't fit your dress and I could. So that's the only reason why she went and told you." I started crying.

"Take my dress off and put it where you found it," Mother said, shaking her head as she left my room.

From the look on Mother's face, at that moment she knew I was gay. As I think back, I believe that's when I honestly knew as well. Unfortunately, Mother did treat me different than my other two siblings. There were many times, suffering from the middle-child syndrome, I felt like Jan Brady.

Mother absolutely adored my older brother Ray, who was sixteen and the spitting image of his father. Ray could do no wrong. I also believed that Mother was still in love with Ray's father, who was in the military and had left when Ray was born and never came back, or so the story goes.

We all had different fathers. I wasn't sure who my father was, except I knew he was white. That's why I was so light and had, as they say, "good hair."

My baby sister's father was a wannabe drug hustler and thug. He would come by and give my mother money to have sex with him. She didn't think I knew, but I was up late one night and I heard them arguing. I heard him tell her that the only reason he gave her money was because she was a good fuck.

The only reason I enjoyed having a baby sister was because she had the toys I wanted to play with, such as dolls, tea cup settings, pink doll houses, and doll clothing. As a boy, Mother wouldn't dare buy girly things like that for me, so I played with Keshia's.

My sister and I always got into arguments because she never wanted me to play with her toys, but yet she always wanted to play house. What kinda shit was that? Like I said, I was older. She was six, and I was eleven. And, of course, when she didn't get her way, she would run to Mother.

I finally stopped playing with her and started playing with my big brother. Hmmm! My brotha, Lawd Jesus.

*

I had just turned twelve when I snuck into Mother's bedroom and took one of her dresses and a pair of her high-heeled shoes and ran back to my room to try them on. Mother had taken Keshia out shopping, and Ray was out hanging with his boys or whatever. I took all my clothes off and stood in the full-length mirror and realized I had a really nice little body. I had a better shape than Mother, to be honest. I had begun puberty, so hair had begun to grow in my private area, and my butt was forming into a nice, smooth apple shape. I stood less than five feet tall and weighed less than eighty pounds.

I slowly put my mother's dress over my head, and the feeling I felt as the dress fell down and hugged my naked body excited me. At the time, I didn't know whether the dress was made of silk or rayon or what, but it felt good against my skin. I didn't get aroused like most boys I had noticed in the shower whose little dicks would get hard. Instead, my excitement was a tingling sensation of a surge that went through my entire body.

I stepped into my mother's high-heeled shoes, which fit perfectly, and nobody couldn't tell me shit as I stood there admiring myself with my light, smooth skin, thick, pink lips, long eyelashes, and curly, black hair.

I was better looking than any girl I knew. Even my

brother's girlfriend, who he thought was all that. Humph, she didn't have anything on me.

I turned on my brother's stereo system and popped in Patti Labelle's CD and lip-synched the words as I looked in the mirror and made up steps as though I was performing.

"Dayum, baby boy! Whatchoo doing?" Ray asked, catching me off guard.

Ray always called me "baby boy." I don't know why. I guess he started calling me that since I was born, and since I was the baby at the time, he just called me baby boy.

"Ah, nothing," I replied, feeling embarrassed and ashamed.

"Does your mother know you going around here wearing her shit?" he asked, changing his clothes.

That's another thing about Ray I didn't understand. We had the same mother, but he always referred to her as "your mother," as though she wasn't his as well.

"Yeah," I lied. I took off Mother's dress as quickly as I could.

"Yeah, I bet." Ray stared at me kinda funny, standing there in his boxers.

"She do. Honest," I stated, trying to sound convincing as I stood there butt naked.

"Yo, baby boy. Wow! You shaped like a honey. Dayum!" he said, walking over to me and looking me up and down in my birthday suit, especially at my ass.

I knew my brother liked what he saw. Like I said, I had a really nice shape. However, I wasn't sure how I really felt about that. After all, we were brothers. But what could I say? He was right.

What really caught me off guard was that he began feeling me on my ass and sliding his middle finger up and down the crack of my ass as he began pulling at himself. I mean, he didn't even ask. No one had ever done that to me, but for some reason, it felt good, really good, even to the point where my knees began to shake.

Suddenly, we heard our mother and Keshia come through the door. Ray stopped and started putting on the rest of his clothes, and I did the same.

For the rest of that evening, we acted as though nothing ever happened. Ray did help me get my mother's dress and shoes back into her closet without her noticing, and then he went out.

I lay in the bed tossing and turning, waiting for him to come home, to see if things would pick up where we left off.

I didn't know what time it was, but Ray finally made it home and had awakened me from my sleep. "Yo, baby boy, wake up," he said, lying on the bunk beneath me.

The room Ray and I shared together was too small for two separate beds, so my mom had bought us bunk beds. I slept on top, and Ray slept on the bottom bunk.

"Yo, baby boy," he whispered again.

"Yeah," I replied, wiping the sleep out of my eyes.

"You awake?"

"Yeah."

"Come down here. I wanna talk to you."

I climbed down from my top bunk and sat alongside his bunk as he slid over, making room on his bed for me.

"What's wrong?" I whispered.

"I just wanted you to know that I know you're gay. You know I know that, right?"He began to take his wifebeater and boxers off while under the covers.

"Yeah," I said, feeling somewhat ashamed.

"Well, look here, baby boy. Don't be ashamed of what you are. But do me one favor. Would you do that for me?" Ray looked like he was high on something, because his eyes were rolling around in his head. And he looked as though he was playing with himself under the covers.

"What's that?"

"I don't want any of my friends, or anybody for that matter, coming up to me, telling me they done fucked my little brother in da ass, a'ight? I don't think I could handle that, a'ight? Promise me." He grabbed on to my arm tightly.

I squealed as I began to feel the pain in my arm. "Okay, I promise."

"A'ight, cool. And I want you to make me another promise."

"Okay," was all I could say.

"If you ever feel the need to want some dick, you come to me. You understand? I'd rather you get it from me than one of my home boys and they throw that shit up in my face. You hear me, baby boy?" he asked, tightening his grip on my arm.

"Yeah, Ray, I hear you," I stated nervously.

"A'ight, cool." Then he asked, "Have you ever seen a naked dude before?"

"I've seen the other boys in my class while taking gym, but that's about it."

"Well, I think you're old enough to see what a man looks like." Ray threw the covers off himself.

Now, I'd never seen my brother totally naked before, but wow, he had a big dick.Or at least a bigger dick than any I'd ever seen. All I could do was stare at it, my mouth hung open. My brother knew he had it going on, and he knew I liked what he was showing me.

"Go ahead, baby boy. Touch it; it won't bite," he whispered, all the while licking his lips and stroking himself.

I knew there was something wrong with this picture, but truth is, I wanted to touch it. I'd never touched a hard dick before, and there was something fascinating about it as Ray continued to stroke himself. Nervously, I reached out and held his hard dick in the palm of my hand. The sensation that traveled through my hand, up my arm, and down my body put a smile on my face that I still carry with me today. And if I didn't know I was gay before then, chile, I knew now.

My brother placed his hand over top of mine and guided my strokes, educating me as to how he liked to be masturbated. Once I caught on to his rhythm, he let go and laid back and began to enjoy the thrill of his little brother bringing him to ecstasy. His moans and groans excited me as I listened and watched his naked masculine body squirm under my control. I'd never seen anybody come before, so when my brother began jerking his body and taking short breaths, and this milky substance shot out from the head of his penis, I thought I had done something wrong and somehow broke his dick. I later found out that a man would do almost anything you want him to do to have that milky substance escape from his manhood. I was glad I had found that out at an early age, and to think that I have my brother to thank for that.

# Chapter 3

Since that night with Ray, he had been treating me a lot better. It's not like he treated me badly before or anything, it's just that he had been spending more time with me and talking with me, you know.

My little sister, however, was getting on my last nerve. Like I said, every time she didn't get her way, she went running to Mother.

"Cameron, why do you keep messing with her?" Mother yelled.

"Mother, I'm not messing with her," I lied. Truth is, I was teasing her by constantly pinching her on the arm as we sat and tried to watch *The Cosby Show*.

"Go to your room," Mother demanded. "And stay in there before I knock the 'cowboy shit' outta you. You're punished until I tell you you can come out."

"Bitch," I whispered under my breath as I stomped to my room.

I closed my door, lay across my bed, and bawled my eyes out. I know it was my fault, that I should have just left Keshia alone, but like I said, she just got on my nerves to the point where I really wanted to hurt her. Not to the point of causing her to go to the hospital or anything, but just enough to make her cry. I think deep down I was jealous because I used to be the baby of the family and used to get all the love she was now getting.

After I cried all the tears I could, I turned on Ray's stereo and played my Patti Labelle CD. I don't know why, but every time I felt down, I would play Patti and I would feel so much better, standing in front of the mirror and making up dances as I lip-synched the words of the song. Of course my mother had to bang on the wall to tell me to turn the music down, but I didn't care, because chile, I was on stage singing to a standing room-only crowd.

*

The next morning, I woke up early, ate my breakfast, and gathered my book bag for school. I was looking forward to going to school lately because our seventh grade class had gotten a new math teacher, Mr. Jamison. And, honey, was he fine. I would sit at the front of the class just so I could get a better look at him and check out the huge print in his pants. I often had to catch myself from staring too long, being afraid that someone would catch me.

I thought to myself, if my brother was as big in the dick department and only sixteen going on seventeen, Mr. Jamison, who I found out was twenty-eight, had to be twice or maybe three times as big, right? After all, I had mastered the art of giving a hand job, so in my mind, I couldn't help but think what it would be like to do the same to this full-grown, fine-ass man.

Now, I may not have been that smart when it came to relationships between men, because I'd never been in one, but I was willing to learn. I had a straight 4.0 GPA and was Mr. Jamison's favorite student. I was the first one in his class in the morning and the last one to leave. I would ask him for additional assignments just so I could spend that much more time with him.   And he would definitely challenge me by giving me twelfth-grade math assignments, which I would always get right, and he would look at me with such pride. At the time, I thought it was love. Humph! Silly me, duh!

Some of the boys in my class would still call me a punk or sissy from time to time, but I was so ahead of them mentally, I paid them no mind. I had began to relate more with the girls in my class and how they felt about these stupid little boys who didn't know the difference between a noun and pronoun, or a verb and an adverb. Well, you get my point.

My best friend in junior high school was this girl named Robin Parker. She knew I was as gay as a pocketbook full of dicks, but she loved me just the same. Robin and I both thought Mr. Jamison was fine, and we would kee-kee and holler on the phone for hours and in person as to who was going to marry him first. A little plump for her size, Robin was my first fag-hag friend. She lived around the corner from me, so we would walk each other to school and home together.

One day as we walked home from school, Robin wanted me to meet her over at the recreational center up the street from where we live, so she could point out this boy she liked so much. She didn't know if he was gay or not, so she wanted me to meet him and pull out my gay radar and let her know if I thought he was gay. I told her I would meet her there, even though my mother had punished me several days before and barred me from coming out of my room, let alone outside. But, hell, I was willing to take a risk, especially when it came to checking out boys.

*

I opened the door and listened to see if anyone was home. I knew my mom would be at work, but I didn't know if Keshia was in her after-school program or over our neighbor's apartment waiting for me to pick her up. As for Ray, he came home when he came home.

I put my book bag down and went next door to see if Keshia was there. "Hello, Ms. Washington. Is Keshia here?" I asked, standing outside the door.

"Good afternoon, Cameron. Yes, your sister is here.

She's been waiting for you." She yelled inside her apartment with the door open, "Keshia, your brother is here!" Then she said to me, "She will be out in a moment. Would you like to come in and wait for her?"

"No, ma'am. Just tell her to come home, and I'll leave the front door unlocked for her."

"Okay, Cameron. You're such a sweet little boy."

God, I hated when Ms. Washington said that. Every time I came there to pick Keshia up, she would say, "You're such a sweet little boy." Humph, if she only knew how sweet.

I went next door to our apartment and waited for Keshia by the door. I was trying to think of a way I could sneak out and meet with Robin, but nothing would come to mind. I thought, *May be I could get Keisha to take a nap. After all, I would only be gone for less than an hour."*

Keshia came running through the door. "Cameron, I'm hungry. Would you fix me a grilled cheese sandwich please?"

"Did you do your homework?"

"Uh-huh. I did it over Ms. Washington house," she replied, throwing her book bag down on the living room couch. "You gonna fix me a grilled cheese sandwich?"

"I'll fix you a grilled cheese sandwich if you promise not to tell Mommy I went to the recreational center."

Keshia smiled. "Okay, I promise."

Within minutes, I had fixed her a grilled cheese sandwich along with a glass of milk and watched as she ate and drank until she was full. I then proceeded to change my school clothes and put on a tight pair of jeans that showed off my small shape, and my favorite blue sweater that fit perfectly.

As I headed to the front door, Keshia said, "Orrr, I'ma tell Mommy."

See, that's why I couldn't stand this little bitch. "Keshia, you said if I fixed you a grilled cheese sandwich that you wouldn't tell," I stated, trying to remind her of our agreement.

"Nah," she replied, flicking out her tongue and running into our mother's bedroom.

I could have run after her, but if I did, I would have punched her in the throat and she wouldn't have been able to say shit. But that would have gotten me in more trouble with Mother.

I didn't know what I was going to do. *Do I stay in, or do I sneak out and have this little bitch run her mouth?*

We lived on the second floor, and I could hear all the other kids outside playing and having fun. It was a warm, sunny day, and inside this apartment was the last place I wanted to be.

I kneeled down and lifted up the window in our living room that faced the square in our neighborhood and watched as the guys played basketball while the girls sat on the bleachers giggling and checking out the guys.

"Yo, Ray, pass me the ball. I'm open," I heard one of the basketball players yell.

"Man, I got this," Ray yelled back, running down the court.

I wasn't a big sports fan, but I did enjoy watching Ray play ball. He was good at any sport he played. He was on the varsity football and basketball team at his school. Not that it was any secret, but the kids in the neighborhood didn't know that Ray and I were even related. I guess that's because I was so light-skinned and he was dark-skinned, and we had different last names. Mine was Jenkins, his was Watson.

Honey chile, I just couldn't take it any longer. This cabin fever was driving me crazy. I had been in this damn house for the past few days and was fucking tired of it.

I closed the window and marched out the front door.

Keshia yelled in the background, "I'ma tell Mommy."

"Go ahead, you rug rat. I don't give a shit!" I climbed down the steps heading to the front door of our apartment complex.

Once I was outside, I felt free. The warmth of the sun shined on my face as I tried to stare at it. Needless to say, I lost that battle, but it felt good.

"Hey, Cameron!" Robin yelled. "Come here."

I looked and saw that Robin had just taken a seat over at the bleachers where the older girls were sitting. As I walked over to where she was, I heard some of the guys around my age whisper, "Punk," and "Sissy," as I switched by. I wasn't bothered by that, but I guess they called me that because of the way I dressed and the way I walked. I had a natural switch as I walked. I think some thought I was doing it on purpose, but I wasn't. That was just how I walked. I couldn't help it. *Jealous bastards!*

"Hey, girl," I said, greeting Robin with two snaps of my finger. I only snapped my finger from time to time because Robin always got a big kick out of it. She said it reminded her of the two gay guys on the TV show *In Living Color*.

"See that guy over there with the red shorts on?" she said, pointing to one of the guys playing basketball with my brother.

"Yeah, girl. Whew, chile," I said, fanning myself.

"That's the guy I was telling you about earlier."

I watched him run up and down the court. "Hmmm. Girl, he is fine, but don't you think he's a little too old for you?"

"No," she replied with attitude.

"Well, he looks to be around seventeen or eighteen, and you're only thirteen. Ms. Thang, what he gonna do with you?"

"Humph. Anything he wants."

We both broke out laughing.

"Girl, I'm skurd of you," I responded, rolling my neck from side to side.

I didn't know what it was, but whenever I was around Robin, the girl in me just came out. I think that's because I could be myself around her, and that's what she expected from me. I didn't dare act this way around my mother. She would've knocked the cowboy shit outta me, as she would say.

Robin whispered in my ear, "Now, all we have to do is get you a boyfriend too."

"Chile, boo," I said, rolling my eyes.

"Hmmm." She pointed at Ray. "I think he would be your

type."

I so wanted to tell Ms. Thang he was my brother, that we slept in the same bed each and every night, that he let me jerk him off from time to time, but I was afraid she might tell somebody, and word would get back to my brother.

The older girls got up from the bleachers and formed a line. They started chanting the name of one of the basketball players, saying, "Junior, Junior, he's our man. If he can't do it, nobody can. Junior, Junior, he's so great, if you make this basket, I'll be your date."

Eventually, Robin got up and started chanting along with the other girls. "Come on, Cameron, join in," she said, waving her hand at me to come join them.

I hopped my little fast yella ass down off the bleachers and joined right in and didn't give it a second thought. After chanting a few times, I began adding some dance steps along with the chanting.

"Junior, Junior, he's our man. If he can't do it, nobody can. Junior, Junior, he's so great, if you make this basket, I'll be your date. Yeah!" I yelled, kicking my legs high in the air. Chile, I just knew I was the shit. None of them bitches had anything on me.

Next thing I knew, Junior came over to where I stood and began cussing me out, calling me, "faggot this," and "faggot that," and then punched me dead in the mouth. My little yella ass fell to the ground so hard, I swore I heard my ass bone crack. I was in so much pain; I didn't know what hurt more, my ass or my mouth. All I could do was lay there and cry.

Suddenly, there was a lot of yelling, and everyone started to gather over by the basketball court. I tried to get up but couldn't. Robin saw that I was having a hard time, and she came over to help.

Once I got up, we got closer to the court, where I saw my brother beat Junior's ass so bad. If Junior's homeboys didn't stop Ray, he would have killed him right then and there.

"Come on, Ray, you made your point, bruh. Go inside

before you get locked up, man," his boy said.

Just then we heard the sound of police sirens coming from all directions.

"You betta run, nigga," Junior said, as he lay on the ground. He spat blood. "I'ma kill yo' ass."

*

That evening before dinner, Mother wanted to know what happened to my lips, swollen from Junior punching me in the mouth. I told her I got in a fight at school. But my sister, with her big mouth, told my mother that I didn't get in no fight at school and that I went outside when I wasn't supposed to and got in a fight on the basketball court.

Mother sent me to my room without dinner and told me she was gonna slap the cowboy shit outta me.

*Whateva.*

I didn't mind being sent to my room, because Ray had stayed in our room since the fight earlier that day. Don't get it twisted, he wasn't hiding out or scared to go outside because of Junior. His boys thought it was best that he stayed in, so five-0 wouldn't find him out on the street and lock him up.

Besides, I was glad he had stayed in, because I wanted to thank him in whatever way I could for standing up for me. He told me whenever I was ready for some dick, to come to him first, right?

# Chapter 4

As I entered our bedroom, Ray was laying across his bunk listening to rap music on his stereo. Personally, I didn't like rap music, but Ray seemed to love it. I climbed up on my bunk without saying a word, because once Ray was into his music, he didn't like to be disturbed.

After thirty minutes or so, Ray turned off his rap music, turned on *The Quiet Storm*, and began conversation.

"Hey, baby boy."

"Yeah."

"What you doin'?"

"Nuf'n."

"Cool, cool."

"Hey, Ray."

"What?"

"Thanks for standing up for me today."

"No problem, baby boy. Ah, can I ask you a question?"

"Yeah."

"Why do bitches get upset with a nigga when other bitches come on to them?"

I never knew why Ray asked me these kinda questions

about the relationship between a man and a woman. I guess he thought that since I only hung around females, I was close to a being a female without being one...if that makes sense.

Lately, he'd been talking to me about his relationship with his girlfriend Jasmine, some hoochie he'd met at some party about six months ago. I call her a hoochie because she barely wore any clothes, wore these big-ass hoop earrings, and was ghetto as hell. I will give her credit for having a nice body. She was about my height, brown skin, small waist, and nice little bubble ass, but of course, her body wasn't as shapely as mine. Anyways, she thought she was all that because her father was a doctor and they lived in a well-to-do neighborhood.

"Yo, baby boy, you fall asleep or sumf'n?"

"No. I was just thinking about your question. So what happened? What did you do?" I knew my ladies' man-brother done probably hit on some other hoochie right in front of Jasmine.

"I ain't do nuf'n. Last weekend I took her to this nice restaurant, and the waitress, a short, sexy honey, started coming on to me, and she got mad at me. And I don't understand that shit. Why do females do that?"

"I guess she thinks you might like her better."

"Like her better? I don't even know her," Ray replied, sounding frustrated.

"I don't know, Ray. Maybe Jasmine thought the waitress was better-looking than her."

"Regardless of that, all I know is, she hasn't given me any pussy since then, and a brotha got needs. Shit!" He grabbed his dick.

I don't know if that was an invitation for me to say something or what. The only thing Ray had allowed me to do was jerk him off, and I don't even know if he had ever thought about sticking his dick in me. I knew he liked the way my butt looked because sometimes when I jerked him off, he would ask me to take my pants off, so he can see my butt while I jerked him off.

"Yo, baby boy," Ray whispered.

"Huh?"

"You ever fucked a girl before?" he asked in a genuine tone.

"Ewww, no." I frowned my face up. Just the thought alone, I felt like throwing up.

"Ah, baby boy, you don't know what you missing, yo," he replied, still pulling on himself. "Dayum, I'm horny as a muthafucka."

I really wanted to feel what it felt like to have a dick in me. Although a part of me was scared, another part of me wanted to experience what Robin had been telling me about. You see, Robin lost her virginity when she was twelve, and she made it sound like the best feeling you could ever have. I felt now was my chance and wasn't about to blow it.

I climbed down off the bed and started taking all my clothes off while my back was facing Ray. As I pulled my drawers down, I bent all the way down to my ankles so he could get a better look between the crack of my virgin ass. His eyes were closed, but I knew he was still awake because, as I looked over my shoulder, his eyelids were fluttering and he began to masturbate.

"Hey, Ray," I whispered.

Ray stopped playing with himself. It was as though he'd fallen asleep, but something told me he was playing possum because no one could fall to sleep that fast.

"Hey, Ray," I whispered again.

Ray moaned and open his legs wide, allowing the covers to fall farther down his torso. I saw his swollen dick laying against his leg. I looked over on the dresser to see what I could use so my butt wouldn't be so dry once I tried to stick his dick up in me. Hopefully it wouldn't hurt as bad. Robin told me that once I decided to let a brotha up in me, make sure they had some Vaseline and a condom. I knew Ray had some condoms, but I didn't know where they were. I really didn't care because it wasn't like he could get me pregnant, and I wasn't worried about no diseases, this being my first time.

**31**

I grabbed the petroleum jelly jar off the dresser and sat it on the floor next to our bunk bed. I climbed in between Ray's legs and pulled the cover all the way off. I kneeled there looking at his beautiful piece of wood throbbing and moving on its own. I reached and grabbed his hard penis and began to slowly move my hand up and down his shaft.

Ray began to moan and squirm like he always did.

After a minute or so of playing with his penis in my hand, I leaned down and placed the tip of his penis in my mouth. As soon as he entered my mouth, his body started to jerk. I knew he was enjoying it. I didn't want him to cum, so I took him out of my mouth.

Once his jerking and breathing had calmed down, I took him in my mouth and this time, I let it go in as far as I could without choking. It was amazing how warm his dick felt in my mouth as I proceeded to go up and down on his manhood.

Suddenly, I began to taste this salty substance coming from him. I knew that was pre-cum, based upon what Robin had told me about her first experience in sucking a dick. And as much as I enjoyed sucking my brother off, my jaws were beginning to hurt. Besides, give me a break…this was my first time sucking a dick.

I then pulled him out of my mouth and began to masturbate him as I leaned over and took a big glob of petroleum jelly and put it up in and around my butt hole. Ray lay there very quietly, but again, I knew he was awake because when I had him in my mouth, I had looked up at him and caught him looking down at me. He then closed his eyes shut real fast, and probably thought I didn't see him.

Once I was sure I had enough petroleum jelly up in my ass, I straddled Ray and slowly began to sit down on him as I guided his dick up in my ass. I barely got the head in and I could feel the pain, but I closed my eyes tight, grit my teeth, and sat all the way down on it.

The pain that shot through me almost caused me to fall out. I'd never felt that kinda pain before. I thought getting banged in the mouth by Junior hurt, but that didn't come close. I sat still, trying to get the pain to go away, or at least that's what Robin told me would happen if I just sat still on it. I also knew I had to relax my ass muscles as much as I could, to help decrease the pain.

Several minutes had gone by, and now the pain I once felt was turning into pleasure. So, I slowly began to move up and down on my brother's manhood.

"Dayum, baby boy! What you doing?" he asked, like he was just waking up from a deep sleep and didn't know what was going on.

I whispered as I looked down into his eyes, "I'm just giving you what you want and need, to say thank you for what you did for me today."

"You know this shit ain't right, baby boy," he whispered as he cupped my ass with the palm of his hands and tried to slide himself up in me as far as his manhood would go.

"You like the way it feels, Ray?" I whispered.

"This ain't right, baby boy," he whispered back, still grinding on my ass.

"That's not what I asked you, Ray," I whispered. I tightened my ass cheeks on his manhood. "I asked you if it felt good."

"Dayum, baby boy! Yeah, you feel real good, baby boy, fa real." Ray looked like he was trying to control his urge to cum.

I always knew when Ray was about to cum. His body would squirm, and then he would take short breaths, and then his body would start jerking, and within seconds he would squirt his nut.

"You ready to nut, big brotha?" I asked, moving up and down on him at a faster pace.

Before Ray could even respond, his body began to squirm, and then he started taking deep breaths, and just like that, he squirted his nut all in me.

I watched the ecstasy on his face as I threw my head

back and felt the ecstasy of having him nut in me.

I began stroking myself the way I'd stroked Ray, and I too climaxed for the very first time. I can't begin to explain how amazing that felt and what an impression it left on me at such a young age.

*

The weeks had flown by. I wanted to be around my big brother every second of the day. Chile, I was so sprung, I hadn't spent any time with my best friend Robin. Every time she called, I gave her the same excuse of being on punishment and not being able to come out. Truth of the matter was, I was hanging around Ray whenever he allowed it. You see, Ray didn't mind me being around because he liked dicking me down.

He even brought me several pairs of female panties to wear, all in different colors. Blue, red, black, yellow, white…you name it, I had it. His favorite color was the yellow panties because I was so light-skinned. He liked the contrast of the yellow panties against my skin. When we were home alone, he would ask me to put them on and put on a fashion show for him. I really enjoyed that because I would play my Patti Labelle CD and "cat-walk" from one side of our bedroom to the other.

Ray would lie on his bunk and play with himself until I tried on every pair, and then he would lean me up against the wall, slide the panties to one side, hawk and spit right in the crack of my ass, and then stick his manhood up in me.

Now, I know you might think that's gross, but trust me, I was getting my life!

Ray and I had fucked so much, I didn't need any Vaseline or much lube at all. Once he would get it in, my ass would start to moist all on its own. Good pussy does make its own juice, children.

Unfortunately, there was a downside.

Ray would feel so guilty after we had sex, he would start to yell at me and say things like, "Get away from me," or "Why you make me do that?"

Chile, boo. Like it was my fault. Yeah, right.

**34**

Then he would go over to his hoochie girlfriend Jasmine's house and try to get with her, so he could still feel like a man. And when she didn't give him any, he would come home and wake me up in the middle of the night, asking if I wanted some more dick.

Of course, I always did. I would never turn Ray down. I loved him because he was my brother, and I loved him because, in my mind, he was my man as well.

# Chapter 5

Ray was going to be graduating from high school within the next few weeks. I wanted to buy him something really special. I didn't know what, but I knew what it would be once I saw it. The problem was, I didn't work, and my mother couldn't afford to give us an allowance. So I started going to the store for people in the neighborhood. I was going to be a teenager in a few more weeks as well, so I was old enough and responsible enough to get what people needed from the store. Hell, aside from that, I was sexually active.

This one day, I went to the store for this lady named Ms. Tracey, who lived across the street from where I lived. She was about twenty-five years old.

When I came back from the store with her groceries, she looked me up and down and said, "Boy, you look good enough to eat."

Now, to tell you the truth, she scared the shit out of me. I thought she was one of those people who ate people. I know, I know, being as grown as I thought I was, you would think I would have known what the ho meant, but I didn't.

I raced home to tell Mother exactly what she'd said to

me. "Mother!" I yelled, running through the door.

"Boy, why you doing all that yelling?"

"Ms. Tracey said I looked good enough to eat." I tried to catch my breath. "Does that mean she eats people?"

"No, it doesn't, Cameron." Mother laughed. "Just don't go in her house when no one else is there."

Anyway, it still didn't make sense to me. I didn't understand why my mother laughed. I went to my room hoping Ray would be in there listening to his rap music and I could ask him, but he wasn't there.

My little sister barged in my room without knocking. "Cameron, you wanna play house?"

"No, I don't wanna play no house. Get outta my room, Ms. Thang." I threw one of my pillows at her.

"Ouch! You hit me in my eye. I'm gonna go tell Mommy." She began to cry, holding her hand up to her eye and running out of my room.

"Good."

To be honest, I did feel a little bad because I hadn't played house with my baby sister in a while. I guess that's because I'd grown up, and putting on a dress and playing the mother no longer interested me, especially now that I knew what dick felt like.

As I lay across my bunk thinking, I remember Ray said that he had a surprise for me on my thirteenth birthday. I couldn't wait for my birthday to come in a couple of days. You would think this was a sick situation for an older brother and a younger brother to be doing the nasty, but I didn't blame Ray for any of it. If anyone was to blame, it was me. I didn't make the first move, but once it was made, I was the one who took it to another level. I was fast as a young queen in training and knew a little too much for my age.

After dinner that evening, my mother asked if I would wash the dishes and clean up the kitchen because she had been in the kitchen all day and was too tired. I really didn't want to because Ray always went flying out the door after dinner and I always followed him. But since I agreed to clean up the kitchen, I didn't have any idea as to where he was.

After cleaning the kitchen, I went door to door of every friend Ray had in our neighborhood looking for him. How sad is that? Chile boo, I was whipped. Anyway, none of his friends had seen or heard from him.

As luck would have it, Ms. Tracey, the cannibal from across the street, saw me heading into my apartment complex.

"Hey, Cameron!" she yelled.

"Yes," I said, turning around and facing her.

"Are you looking for your brother Ray?"

"Yeah, I am," I replied while walking over in her direction.

"He's in here playing cards with my brothers." She looked me up and down, holding the door open so I could enter.

Ms. Tracey still lived at home with her mother and her two younger brothers, Rocky, a year older than Ray, and Jack, who was the same age. Jack was into playing basketball and football like Ray.

I entered their house and found the three of them in the living room playing the card game, truth or dare.

"Dayum, yo! I see your little brother still follow you everywhere you go, Ray." Rocky started laughing.

"Yo, little man, you wanna play some truth or dare with us?" Jack asked.

"Sure. Why not?" I sat down next to my brother.

"You sure you wanna play, baby boy?"

"Yeah, I'm sure. I'm old enough," I spat with a little attitude.

"Well, okay." Ray began to deal the cards.

"Now, how do you play this game?" I asked, picking up my cards.

"It's just a game of tunk." Rocky picked up his cards. "Have you ever heard of it?"

"Nope, but I'ma fast learner, if someone explain it to me," I said, smiling and rocking from side to side.

"Yo, Ray, your little brother is a trip, man," Rocky teased.

Jack began explaining the game to me, and it really didn't seem all that difficult. Of course, I didn't win any of the games we played, but I was a trooper and took my dare like a man. Yeah, right!

Anyway, Ms. Tracey happened to walk by and noticed that I was playing the truth or dare game and asked if she could join in. I really didn't know what they were up to, but they started laughing and smiling amongst themselves, including my own brother.

It was my turn to deal the cards, so I picked them up and shuffled them a few times and began to deal them out. Before the game had even started, it was over when Ray threw his hand down and yelled twenty-one. He had the lowest hand, so he won that round.

"Truth or dare?" he asked me.

"Dare," I said with attitude.

He hesitated and looked around at Rocky, Jack, and Ms. Tracey, and they all looked back at him, smiling and nodding their heads. He then turned to me and said, "I dare you to go upstairs and take all your clothes off and get in Tracey's bed." He looked at me with a straight face.

"You want me to what?" I asked as though I didn't hear him the first time.

"You heard me. I want you to go upstairs and take all your clothes off and get in Tracey's bed.

I didn't understand why my brother wanted me to do that, but I couldn't resist because, if I did, each of them could punch me ten times each. And, personally, I didn't think Rocky liked me that much. He was already rubbing his fists together, warming them up to hit me.

Before I headed upstairs to perform my dare, my brother turned to Ms. Tracey and said, "Truth or dare?"

"Dare," she said, smiling from ear to ear.

"I want you to go upstairs and take all your clothes off

**40**

and get in bed with my little brother."

Ms. Tracey didn't waste any time going upstairs to her room. As a matter of fact, she passed me going up the steps. Anywho, if I didn't know any better, I would say they had planned this because they were laughing and giving each other high-five and shit.

I slowly continued to walk up the steps, while my brother and his friends followed. I walked in Ms. Tracey's room, and she was already in the bed waiting for me. I closed the door, but this was one of those old houses where above the door was a glass window. My brother and his friends climbed on a chair and looked in to make sure I performed my dare.

I took all my clothes off, jumped in Ms. Tracey's bed, and pulled the covers over me.

Rocky yelled through the window, "Yo, shawty, you got to get on top of her for at least sixty seconds. That's a whole minute."

I looked at my brother, hoping he would get me out of this terrifying ordeal, but he was nodding his head and clapping along with Rocky.

"Yeah, baby boy, don't be scared. It won't hurt."

So, believing it wouldn't hurt, like my brother said, I climbed on top of Ms. Tracey. Then she suddenly wrapped her arms around my small waist, squeezed me tightly, threw her legs wide open in the air, and began to grind her body against mine.

Now, I wasn't stupid. I knew this was my brother's way of getting me my first piece of pussy. And even though I didn't know what I was doing, I began to grind back. It was hard for me to get an erection while thinking about what I was doing with Ms. Tracey, but once I started thinking freaky and imagining I was having sex with my brother and his friends, that's when my little dick started to get hard. I was a true gay young freak. What can I say?

I didn't know what hole my dick was to go in, so I raised up off her so she could guide it in herself. Once it was in, it felt kinda funny. It's hard to explain, but I humped up and down, in and out, until I actually found myself getting excited enough to cum. I didn't know if Ms. Tracey had cum or not. She did shake a little, but that don't mean anything.

After several minutes of humping and listening to the sounds that my brother and his friends made, cheering me on, I came inside of Ms. Tracey. *Ewww!* And for the record, I didn't enjoy it at all. Chile, I thought I was gonna throw up. My stomach began to do flips that scared the shit out of me. Nausea had set in something fierce. I thought I could hold my illness back, but I couldn't.

As soon as I rose up off the bed, I bent over and hurled all over Ms. Tracey's bed. Chile, I was so embarrassed, I didn't know what to do. I looked over at my brother, expecting his support, but he began to roll with laughter, as did his friends.

Ms. Tracey, on the other hand, didn't think it was funny at all. She jumped up out of the bed as I hurled and began fussing at how I'd just ruined her bed sheet and spread.

I put my clothes on and bolted out of there so fast, you would have thought I was running for my life.

As soon as I got to my room, I took all my clothes off and jumped in the shower. I closed my eyes as I stood under the shower and thought about what had just happened. I actually got my first piece of pussy, but it didn't make me feel more like a man. As a matter of fact, I felt dirty and grimy.

I remember Ray telling me that it was so good that I didn't know what I was missing, but now that I'd had it, I really didn't think I was missing anything at all. I still preferred the masculinity and the body of a man.

I finished my shower and went to my room and cried myself to sleep.

\*

I was awakened by Ray as he stood alongside my bunk. "So you got your first piece of pussy, baby boy," he said. "What do you think?" He started taking off his clothes.

"What do you think, Ray? I threw up? What do you think I think?"

"Dayum, baby boy! That was messed up, too." Again he roared with laughter as he lay down on his bunk.

"Dayum what?"

"I just thought you would enjoy it. That's all."

"It was sickening, Ray. That's what it was. Remember, you were the one that told me to be who and what I am. And if I needed to be with someone, you wanted that someone to be you, remember?" I waited for his response.

"Dayum! Baby boy, you really like dick more, huh?"

"So, y'all planned that, huh?" I asked, avoiding his question.

"You know, every time I go over there, she's always asking me about you. So, I knew she liked you. So I thought, Why not? It's about time you got some pussy."

He stopped laughing once he realized I wasn't laughing along with him.

"Look, baby boy, I didn't mean any harm, so if I did sumf'n wrong, my bad," he said, sounding somewhat sincere.

"I still enjoy being with you more."

"That's cool, that's cool, but, baby boy?"

"Huh?" I looked down from my bunk to his.

"Make sure you keep that shit between us, a'ight?" He yawned and rolled over to go to sleep.

"Okay," I whispered, feeling a little disappointed that he was going to sleep.

I couldn't wait to go to school tomorrow so I could tell Robin I actually got some girl pussy and the shit made me puke.

\*

"Ms. Thang, I had some girl pussy yesterday," I hollered, trying to convince Robin as we sat in the school cafeteria eating our lunch.

"See, you oughta stop lying. Ain't no girl out here would wanna give you none of their stuff. Don't even try it." Robin rolled her neck at me.

"I did, and FYI, it was a twenty-five-year-old grown woman, so there." I rolled my neck back at her and snapped my fingers in her face.

"Are you serious, fa real?"

"Fa real."

"Do you swear on your little gay life?" she asked, holding up her pinky finger.

I crossed my pinky finger with hers. "I swear on all my Patti Labelle CDs."

Robin knew when we pinky-swore, that meant all jokes aside and that we were telling the truth about whatever we were talking about.

She hollered, "OMG, you're serious?"

"I told you, chile."

"Oooo! Who was this twenty-five-year-old woman? And how did this happen?"

Once I began explaining how I had gone looking for my brother and that he was over the lady's house that said she wanted to eat me, Robin started drooling at the mouth. After telling her the whole story, she looked at me and started laughing hysterically.

"What's so dayum funny, Ms. Thang?" I asked with attitude.

"I'm sorry, sista, but you were basically raped and then threw up."

"Chile, I wasn't raped. I did throw up, but can I help it because she wanted all this?" I performed my "cat-walk" as I headed to my next class.

"Whateva," she spat as the bell rang.

Fortunately, my next class was gym, and fine-ass Mr. Jamison was filling in for our regular gym teacher, who was out sick with the flu. Finally, I was gonna get a chance to see Mr. Jamison in his gym shorts.

I walked in the locker room and began changing into my gym clothes when Mr. Jamison walked in the locker room and

**44**

announced, "Listen up, fellas. We're gonna be swimming today, so just put your gym shorts on."

I wasn't a swimmer. As a matter of fact, I couldn't even remember the last time I went swimming. However, looking at Mr. Jamison with just his swim trunks on and a wind breaker jacket he had open down to his navel, I was willing to be his first drowning victim so he could perform mouth to mouth on me. Ooo, chile, my nerves.

"Okay, fellas, I need y'all to form a line right over here," Mr. Jamison said as we all walked into the pool area. "Now, does anyone know how to tread water?"

Several of the boys raised their hands, but a few of us didn't.

"Okay, all those who know how to tread water, I want you guys on this side of the pool, and those that don't, I want you on this side of the pool. A'ight, fellas, you guys on this side of the pool that can tread, I want you one at a time to swim the length of the pool like this."

Fine-ass Mr. Jamison then took his jacket off, and I almost died. His body was so OMG. His muscles had muscles, and his legs and thighs were that of a Greek god. He was so tone and tight, he didn't have a six-pack, he had an eight-pack.

He stood at the edge of the pool and dove right in the water. He swam to the other side of the pool, did a backflip, and swam back to where we were standing.

When he lifted himself out of the pool, I couldn't believe my eyes. His trunks had come off. I thought I would faint. My knees became weak, and I felt myself become aroused. I quickly placed my hands in front of me, so no one would notice.

Mr. Jamison dived back in the water to retrieve his trunks, but before he did, I noticed he was seriously packed in the front *and* in the back.

Of course, most of the guys started laughing. I, on the other hand, had visions of Mr. Jamison making love to me in the pool right then and there. After all, the only other man I had ever been with was my brother, and now knowing what fine-ass Mr.

Jamison looked like butt naked, I was going to do my best to have him at any cost.

Mr. Jamison tried to show those of us who didn't know how to tread water by holding us up under water as we lay across his arms and splashed our legs around. When it was my turn, I played the helpless victim, to the point of pretending I was drowning.

Mr. Jamison dived under water and held me in his arms as he brought me to the top. As he grabbed me by my small waist and I held on to him, I was fully erect. I knew he felt it as it rubbed up against his stomach. He just looked at me kinda strange and just smiled. I didn't understand what that smile meant, but I was glad he didn't make me feel bad or embarrass me in front of the class. From that point on, I was willing to do anything Mr. Jamison asked of me.

# Chapter 6

My thirteenth birthday fell on the same day as my brother's prom night, so there was definite cause for celebration in our house. My mother actually took the day off just so she could spend the day with me, taking me out to Wantons Bridge Mall, which had just opened up a few blocks away from where we lived.

"Oooo, Mother, can I get these pair of jeans?"

"Cameron, I just bought you a pair of jeans in the other store."

"I know, Mother, but these are better because they have these designs on them. See?" I showed my mother the designs on the back of the jeans.

"Okay, Cameron, but if we get these instead, we gonna have to return the ones I just bought you," Mother said, her hands on her hips.

"Okay, Mother, we can take 'em back now."

Mother purchased my new designer jeans, and then we headed out to return the old ones. As we were walking through the mall, I noticed these guys from in my class, and we were walking towards them. I knew something was going to happen, because they didn't like me and always called me names.

Sure enough, as we walked by them, one of them said, "Faggy," and they all broke out laughing.

I was so hurt and embarrassed, I didn't know what to do. It was the first time anyone had called me a name with my mother within earshot. I lowered my head and looked down at the tile floor as we continued to walk through the mall. I was grateful Mother didn't respond even though I know she heard the derogatory comment.

We returned the jeans, and then we stopped at the food court to grab something to eat. Other than the comment made earlier, I was having a good time hanging out with my mom.

"Mother, I still got to get sumf'n for Ray's prom tonight," I said, as I ate my Big Mac.

"So, what do you wanna get him?" she asked eating her fish filet sandwich.

"I don't know, Mother. I've saved up almost twenty dollars, and I'd like to get him sumf'n nice. May be sumf'n he can wear to his prom."

"Well, they have a lot of jewelry stands in the middle of the mall. Maybe you can get him a chain or something."

"Oh, wow, Mother! That's a great idea. Ray loves those chains with all the bling-bling on them."

After we finished our meal, we stopped at the first jewelry stand we came to. They had this huge 24-inch silver chain with a diamond-studded *R* on it, which I thought was great, and it was only $19.95. I begged my mom for a dollar to help pay the total price, including taxes, and had it gift-wrapped.

I couldn't wait to get home so I could give it to Ray. Now, I knew it wasn't real silver or real diamonds, but who would really know?

*

We finally made it home just a little after seven p.m. It was a warm night. Most of the time, people were usually outside on their patios enjoying the weather, but tonight no one was out, and it was quiet for some reason.

I opened our front door, and it was total darkness. I reached for the switch on the side of the wall to turn on the living room light. To my surprise, practically everyone in the neighborhood was there in my living room, including my best friend Robin. They all shouted, "Surprise" and began singing happy birthday to me. No wonder my mom kept me out all day.

I found out that my mom had given our neighbor, Ms. Washington, the key to our apartment when she dropped my little sister off at her place to watch, since we were going out.

I thanked everyone who was there and gave Robin a big kiss on the cheek. I then began looking for Ray, so I could give him his prom gift, anxious to see what he had bought me.

I went into our bedroom and found him standing in front of our full-length mirror, putting his tuxedo on and admiring himself. "You're forgetting sumf'n," I said, standing behind him while he posed in the mirror.

"And what's that, baby boy?"

"Your gift." I handed him his gift.

I stood and watched as he opened his gift. I guess he must have really liked it because, as soon as he put it on, he walked over to me and kissed me right in the mouth, tongue and everything. This was the first time Ray had ever kissed me. Through everything we had done, I had tried kissing him before, but he'd always turn away and say that was way too gay for him and that would be wrong. I know, right? Whateva.

"Wow," I replied once he was through.

He handed me a small unwrapped box. "Don't tell anybody I did that shit, a'ight?"

I opened the box and saw a joint inside. I didn't smoke and had never tried smoking weed before, so I really didn't understand what this was for.

"Ray, what do you want me to do with this?"

"I want you to stay up until I come home. We gonna smoke it together. I'm gonna give you your birthday present then."

"Ain't you going to the prom with Jasmine?"

**49**

"Yeah. What's the problem?"

"But ain't you gonna do it to her?" I knew I sounded pathetic.

"Probably. Why?"

"Well, Ray, I don't want you to do it to her and then come home and do it to me."

"How you know I'm gonna do it to you when I come home?"

I was so angry, I couldn't believe what came out of my mouth. "If you don't, I'ma tell Mommy what you been doing to me," I said, my arms folded and my lips poked out.

Before I had a chance to move, Ray grabbed me by my collar, threw me on the floor, and slapped me several times in the face. "If you ever tell anybody, I will hurt you so bad, you'd wish you were dead."

I had never seen Ray so angry, except for the time he beat up Junior on the basketball court. To be honest, I was so sorry I said that because I really didn't mean it. I hated that Ray was mad with me, especially on my birthday.

"Ray, I'm sorry. I didn't mean it," I pleaded as he kneeled over me, deciding whether or not to hit me again.

After contemplating a few seconds, Ray then got up and walked out of our bedroom. I got up as fast as I could and walked out into the living room where everyone was eating and enjoying my birthday party.

"There's the birthday boy." Ms. Washington kissed me on the cheek and wished me happy birthday. "Where you been hiding?"

"Thank you, Ms. Washington, but I had to go to the bathroom."

I watched my mom take a few pictures of Ray with his tuxedo on.

"My baby has grown up, and good-looking as ever," she said proudly as she snapped picture after picture of Ray.

"Okay, Mother, that's enough." Ray kissed Mother on the forehead and exited the apartment. "I gotta go."

I tried my best to have fun at my own birthday party, but I couldn't stop thinking about how mad Ray was with me. Robin tried to cheer me up, but I still couldn't get over what I'd said to Ray. Even worse, I couldn't stop thinking about what he'd said about hurting me. The look in his eyes scared the shit out of me.

Robin and I hung out in the kitchen because I really didn't feel like partying and hanging with all the others, even though it was my party.

"Look, Ms. Thang, what's going on with you? You are walking around here being sad and everything. Did somebody say sumf'n bad to you? Who was it? I'll cuss 'em out," Robin said, rolling her neck, her hands on her hips.

"No, nobody said anything bad to me. I guess I'm just not feeling well."

"Po thang. Is my baby having her first period?" Robin whispered, and then she started laughing.

"Chile boo, ain't nobody having no period," I replied, snapping my fingers. "Besides, that was last week, bitch."

We both broke out laughing.

I couldn't wait until my birthday party was over, so I could just go to my room and wait for Ray to come home.

My mother yelled, "Cameron!"

"Ma'am," I yelled back from the kitchen.

Mother grabbed me by the hand and dragged me into the living room, where the music was playing. "Come on and dance with me."

I hated when my mother started drinking. Don't get me wrong, she wasn't an alcoholic or anything, but when she drank, she always wanted me to show her the latest dances. I must admit, I knew all the latest dances, but teaching my mother how to dance was like teaching her algebra. She didn't know how much two plus two was and had two left feet.

Besides, I really wasn't in the mood to dance, although dancing usually made me feel better when I was feeling down. My mother made it hard to say no while everyone stood around waiting for me to dance with her.

I started feeling the music as it played, and my body finally got into it. Before I knew it, I was bumping, grinding, and doing all the latest dances as my mom tried to copy my every move. I was definitely feeling better as I shook my ass around the dance floor. I knew some of the girls were jealous because none of them could dance as well as I could. Most people thought I danced like a girl, but I didn't care. Dancing made me feel free and alive.

When I heard the crowd chant, "Go Cameron, go Cameron, it's yo' birthday, it's yo' birthday," I really started to get into it, doing splits and everything.

Some of the guests had to move. *Outta my way, bitches*, I thought to myself as I vogued and cat-walked up and down my living room floor. And as much as I was enjoying the attention because all eyes were on me, I also wanted to make a statement. If our guests didn't know I was gay before, they would surely know now.

Finally, the party came to an end around midnight, and Mother started putting people out, saying she had to get her beauty sleep. I didn't mind because I was looking forward to the party that Ray and I was gonna have once he got home. And even though I knew he was gonna be with that hoochie girlfriend of his, I still wanted to feel him inside me.

Once everyone had left and my mom and I cleaned up the mess in the apartment, I went to my room, took all my clothes off, and took a hot shower. Just to be ready when Ray got home, I oiled my body down so it could be nice and soft. I also squirted some of the oil up my ass so it could be somewhat lubricated. I then put on one of my cut-off T-shirts that showed most of my stomach, and my yellow panties that Ray got me, his favorite.

# Chapter 7

I didn't know what time it was, but I was startled out of my sleep when I heard someone banging on our living room door. I jumped up out of my bed and went into my mother's bedroom to wake her.

"Mother, somebody at the door," I whispered, tapping on her shoulder.

"What?"

"Somebody at the door."

"Go check and see who it is. It might be Ray. He must have forgotten his key." She rolled over to go back to sleep.

I tiptoed into the living room and peeked out the peephole to see if I could see who it was, but no one was standing there.

"Who is it?" I asked nervously.

"This is Officer Crawley. Is this the home of Mrs. Wilson?"

"Yeah."

"Can I speak with her, please?"

"Wait a minute."

I ran back into Mother's bedroom and whispered,

"Mother, there's a police at the door."

"What da hell! What he want?" she asked, wiping the sleep out of her eye.

I shrugged my shoulders. "He didn't say. He just asked to speak to you."

Mother got out of bed, put her robe on, and headed for the front door. I followed her.

"Can I help you?" she asked through the door.

"Yes, Mrs. Wilson. This is Officer Crawley. Can I come in?"

"What is this in regards to?"

"Are you Raymond Watson's mother?"

"Yes, I am." Mother opened the front door. "Please come in."

"Thank you, madam," Officer Crawley responded as he walked into our living room.

"Is there something wrong with Ray?" Mother asked nervously.

"Well, Mrs. Wilson, would you mind if I sit down?"

"Yes, I do mind," Mother said, getting upset. "Now, I asked you if there was something wrong with my child."

"Well, madam, there was a disturbance at Jefferson High School this evening, and we were called in. Gunshots were fired, and a Mr. Raymond Watson along with another young man was rushed to emergency a little while ago."

"Oh God, no, not my child!" Mother's legs gave out.

Officer Crawley caught her just in time. "Easy, Mrs. Wilson." Officer Crawley tried to seat my mother on the couch.

"No, no, no, this can't be happening." Mother started rocking herself back and forth.

"Mrs. Wilson, I know this is very difficult for you, but your son has been taken to Mt. Sinai Hospital. If you would like a ride there, I'll be more than happy to take you."

"I want to," I stated as firmly as I could.

"Okay, Officer Crawley, I would appreciate that." Mother wiped the tears rolling down her cheeks. "Cameron, go wake up your sister, and see if Ms. Washington will watch her while we go check on your brother."

*

Within twenty minutes we pulled up in front of the hospital in Officer Crawley's cruiser, and Mother and I jumped out and headed towards the information desk.

"Excuse me, my son was brought here about an hour ago," Mother said hysterically. "Can you please tell me where I can find him?"

"Okay, madam, now calm down and tell me what your son's name is."

"His name is Raymond Watson," Mother said, sounding out of breath.

After a few minutes of punching keys on the computer, the receptionist informed us that a Mr. Raymond Watson was brought in about an hour or so ago and was being prepped for surgery, and his doctor was Dr. Ross.

"And where can I find this Dr. Ross?" Mother began tapping her right foot.

"He's with your son in room 316. Once you sign in, you can take the elevator, located here on the left, go to the third floor, and make a right.

Mother signed us both in on a sheet of paper attached to a clipboard, and the receptionist then gave us passes to enter the third floor.

As we rode up in the elevator Mother kept praying out loud and saying the same thing over and over, "Oh Lord, please, don't take my son from me."

As we exited the elevator, we made a right and came across a sign with double doors that read "Intensive Care Unit." As we opened the double doors, I began counting down the room numbers. Ray's room was the last one on the right-hand side.

I reached out and grabbed Mother's hand as we entered the room, and what I saw made me want to puke. Mother immediately began to cry. All I could do was just stare at Ray because I had never known anyone who had been shot. They had tubes coming in and out of his body, tubes up his nose, down his throat, and his face, swollen twice its size, was unrecognizable. If it weren't for the chain I'd bought him and the tuxedo he wore, I would not have known that this young man was my brother.

Dr. Ross turned to face us. "Excuse me, can I help you?"

"Yes, I'm Mrs. Wilson," Mother said through tears as she approached Ray. "This is my son."

Honey, I felt so weak, I couldn't seem to take another step. I stood with my back against the wall, my head hung low. I wasn't sure why, but I was afraid of this man lying on the bed unconscious and fighting for his life. I knew this was my brother, but because of the way he looked, as far as I was concerned, he was a complete stranger. My little body began to shake uncontrollably and lower itself to the floor.

"Hello, Mrs. Wilson, I'm Dr. Ross," he replied, extending his hand.

Mother never bothered to shake Dr. Ross' hand because her focus was on Ray. "Is he gonna be all right, doctor?" she asked, tears flowing as she held Ray's right hand.

"I wish I could answer that, Mrs. Wilson, but I can't." Dr. Ross continued to examine Ray.

Mother yelled, "What do you mean, you can't?"

"Mrs. Wilson, your son has sustained a serious gunshot injury, and to be honest, even if we go in and try to retrieve the bullet, there's no guarantee he will survive it."

"And if you don't operate?" Mother asked, sounding defeated.

Dr. Ross replied softly, "He will surely die."

Once Dr. Ross told Mother that Ray would die if they didn't operate, she instantly fainted. Dr. Ross pressed the emergency button, and other doctors and nurses came running in the room. They placed Mother up on a gurney and rolled her out of the room.

I stayed curled up against the wall not knowing whether to cry, pray, or scream. Once they rolled Mother out of the room, I stood up and tiptoed over to this stranger lying on his back, fighting for his life, on life support, and tubes running in and out of his mouth and up his nose. The tears started to flow down my cheeks. I realized that even if my brother did survive the operation, he would never be the same Ray I knew and loved.

I leaned my head down on his chest just so I could feel closer to him and to listen to his heartbeat. I was wishing I hadn't made him mad before going to his prom. I wanted to take it all back.

I whispered in his ear, "I'm so so sorry for what I said, Ray. I really didn't mean any of it. Please, don't die."

Suddenly, the machine Ray was hooked up to began beeping loudly, and the next thing I know, doctors and nurses were coming from everywhere. I was pulled to the side as I watched them pull out these electric paddles and rubbed them together.

Someone yelled, "Clear," as they slammed these paddles against my brother's chest.

"Leave my brother alone!" I yelled, not realizing they were only trying to keep him alive.

One of the doctors yelled, "Get him outta here."

One of the male nurses picked me up and forcefully carried me out into the hallway. He was trying to explain to me that they were doing everything in their power to help my brother, but I was too busy looking into the glass room as they continued to slap Ray with those electric paddles. I guess I was a little hysterical because the brotha grabbed me so hard, I couldn't help but focus on what he was saying.

"We are doing everything we can to help your brother," he yelled. "Please give us a chance to do that."

"Why are they slapping him with them paddles if they were trying to help him?" I spat, my hands on my hips.

"Those paddles help his heart beat," he tried to assure

me.

"How so?"

"Well, you see sometimes when the heart stops beating, we use those paddles to give an electrical shock to the heart that makes it start beating again."

"Are you saying my brother's heart stopped beating?" I asked, crying again.

At that moment, I saw my mother come running down the hallway. I guess someone must have gone to get her, but she started crying hysterically once she entered my brother's room.

I didn't know what was going on, so I went into the room and stood against the wall just in time to hear one of the doctors say to my mother, "I'm sorry, Mrs. Wilson, but we did all we could."

I wasn't sure what was said after that because everything seemed to have come to a standstill.

Mother threw herself on Ray's body and started screaming, "Wake up, Ray, wake up!"

Dr. Ross tried to console Mother, but she wasn't having it. Mother paid Dr. Ross no mind as she continued to pull and grab at Ray's dead body.

I became numb to everything as I watched my mother hold on to Ray. My dead brother. That sounded so strange to me. A brother that I loved, and was in love with.

I watched as the hospital staff literally had to pry my mother's grip from Ray's dead body before placing a sheet over his head. This was the first time I'd ever experienced this much hurt. Even thinking about it now, brings tears to my eyes.

After Mother said her good-byes to my brother, we walked out of his room arm in arm. I didn't know who was supporting whom, but I guess we were supporting each other.

"I'm sorry for your loss, Mrs. Wilson," Officer Crawley said in a genuine tone as he waited to take us back home.

"Thank you," Mother said through her pain and tears.

As we got into Officer Crawley's cruiser, Mother asked, "Officer Crawley, do you know who did this to my boy?"

"Yes, we have him in custody as we speak, and he will be sent to prison. You can count on that."

"I want to see the monster that killed my boy."

"I don't think now is a good time, Mrs. Wilson. Maybe another time would be better?"

"I want to see the monster that killed my boy!" Mother demanded.

*

Officer Crawley had taken my mother and I down to the police station, where we were informed that the monster, as my mother called him, was still being questioned by an officer in one of the investigation rooms. My mother and I were escorted to another room with a huge mirror on one side of the wall, adjoining the room where the monster was being questioned.

My mouth literally opened wide when I saw who the monster was. How could I tell my mother that the monster who killed her son was the dude on the basketball court named Junior, who Ray beat up because of me? My legs buckled, and this time, I fell straight to the floor.

"Son, are you okay?" Officer Crawley asked as he helped me up.

My eyes began to water once more. "Yeah, I'm fine."

"What is his name?" Mother asked.

Officer Crawley looked at his paperwork. "His name is Jerome Rogers, but they call him Junior."

"He's just a baby himself. How old is he?" Mother asked.

"He just turned eighteen."

As Mother and Officer Crawley talked, all I could do was to stare at Junior behind the glass mirror. The guilt I felt was horrible. Why did I have to go outside that day? If I'd stayed in the house like I was supposed to, Ray would still be alive. How was I supposed to live with this guilt for the rest of my life?

*

Mother and I were chauffeured back to our home, courtesy of Officer Crawley. There wasn't any conversation along the way. Once we got home, Mother went to her room, and I went to mine. I closed my door and lay on Ray's bunk while listening to Mother bawl her eyes out in the next room. As I lay there, I could still feel and smell him all around me.

*Am I sleeping?* I asked this because it felt like a dream. *Am I breathing? Is it my brother who died, or was it me?* I thought it must have been me because my brother had always protected me, so who was going to protect me now? My brother loved me, so who was going to love me now?

I didn't think I could take this kind of pain. *How can I kill myself?* I so wanted to die but was too afraid of death. *How can I go on when I don't want to live? Who will protect me now? What about my brother's clothes and his things? I think I wanna move. I can't stay here in this room and not have my brother here to love me.*

My brother protected me, but he was killed because of me. *I killed my brother. Can anybody hear me? I killed my brother. Wake up, Cameron. This can't be happening. Wake up. I want to kill Junior. Who will protect me now?*

I needed someone to protect and love me. I wanted him to be Beautiful, Black, Employed, Attractive, Understanding, Tall, Independent, Faithful, Unique, Lovable, and most of all, protective of me. Please God, Just Make Him Beautiful.

\*

The following day I didn't wake up until noon time. I really didn't feel like getting up because I had slept in Ray's bed all night, which comforted me.

I got up and walked out into the living room, but all the lights were still out. I went to Mother's room and knocked on her bedroom door, but there was no answer. I quietly opened the door and found her lying in bed, still asleep.

"Mother, wake up," I said, tapping her. She didn't budge or make a sound. "Mother, wake up."

"Leave me alone."

"Mother, it's after twelve o'clock. Didn't Dr. Ross ask you to give him a call around this time?"

"Leave me alone, I said."

"Mother, you have to wake up. We have to make arrangements for Ray."

"I don't have to do a damn thing," she said, turning over and going back to sleep.

I closed Mother's door, got dressed, and went next door to get my baby sister.

I knocked on Ms. Washington's door and waited until she answered.

"Good afternoon, Cameron. So, how is Ray doing?"

Obviously, she hadn't heard. I didn't know how to say it, so I just blurted out, "He's dead. That's how he's doing!" I started to cry again.

"Oh my God!Cameron, I didn't know. Come on in, baby." She opened the door so I could enter.

I walked into her apartment and found Keshia sitting at the kitchen table eating a peanut butter and jelly sandwich with a glass of milk. I sat at the kitchen table and explained to Ms. Washington what had happened when we got to the hospital the night before, and that Ray had died because of me.

"No, Cameron, don't say that. Ray died because it was just his time.God called him, and when God calls, you must answer."

I didn't tell Ms. Washington that Ray had beaten this guy up because of me and that the guy sought out revenge and shot Ray several times in the chest. I thought I would just keep that to myself, but the guilt was still eating me inside, and all I could do was cry. Once I started crying, Keshia started crying as well.

Ms. Washington held and rocked us both. I guess all I really needed was to be comforted by a mother figure because my own mother was so out of it herself that she didn't take into consideration her other two children. I don't mean that in a bad way because I couldn't imagine what a parent must feel like when they lose a child.

*

Finally, Keshia and I went home, only to find Mother still in the bed with the curtains drawn and in the dark. I asked her if she wanted something to eat, but she refused. I fixed Keshia and me a couple of TV dinners, and afterwards I put her to bed.

I sat in the living room alone and in the dark, afraid of what was happening to my family. I had cried so much, my eyes were bloodshot-red, and I was just tired of crying, tired of the pain.

"Please, God, take this pain away," I begged, crying and rocking myself to sleep.

# Chapter 8

Three days after Ray's death, Mother was still in her room, lying in her bed in the dark. My baby sister did nothing but cry and complain about everything I did. Either I wasn't combing her hair the right way, or the food I tried to cook didn't taste right. I was thirteen years old, and I felt like dying. I guess that's why Mother hadn't gotten out of bed. Losing a child just ain't right. God must've been angry at what my brother and I did. I suspected it was only a matter of time before God came for me.

I was so scared that every time the phone rang, I jumped. And the phone had been ringing off the hook. If it wasn't Mother's job calling, it was Dr. Ross calling to see when Mother was coming down to the morgue to have my brother's body moved to a funeral home.

Neither I nor my baby sister had been to school since Ray's death. Fortunately, Ms. Washington had been watching Keshia during the day while I kept an eye on Mother. The problem was, I couldn't get her out of bed or to eat, no matter how hard I tried.

The following day, I sent Keshia over to Ms. Washington's apartment and prepared a hot breakfast for Mother. I cooked scrambled eggs, bacon, and toast, and prepared a glass of cherry Kool-Aid.

I placed it all on a tray and entered Mother's bedroom. "Mother, wake up. I've fixed you some breakfast.Come on, get up." I placed the tray on the bed and turned on the lamp on the dresser next to the bed. She didn't move. "Mother, wake up."

"Leave me alone," she spat.

"Mother, you have to eat sumf'n," I pleaded.

"I don't have to do a damn thing," she stated angrily. "Now, get out of my room."

"No, Mother, I can't do that. Every day you tell me to get outta your room, but today I'm not. I want you to eat sumf'n."

"Who do you think you're talking to? And who the hell are you?"

"I'm your son, that's who I am."

"Son, for your information my son just died. I don't have a son no more. I have a daughter and a faggot. That's what I got left."

I was so shocked, I just froze. I couldn't believe my own mother had said that.

"Now, get the hell outta my room!" she yelled, and turned away from me.

I picked up the tray of food, walked out of the room, and slammed her bedroom door. I was so angry and hurt, I threw the tray of food against the living room wall. It never really bothered me when other people called me names like that, but coming from my own mother, it stung deeply. It was the first time I felt my mother wished I had never been born.

I sat down on the living room couch and cried like a baby. I didn't have my big brother to protect me, and now I didn't have a mother to nurture me. Why was God being so cruel?

One week after Ray's death, Mother still lay in her bed, starving herself in the dark. I believe Mother was trying to kill herself. I really didn't care if she did. The pain and the hurt that I once felt had now turned to anger. I was mad at everything and everyone…Mother, Junior, and especially God. The best thing about my anger was, it helped me to stop crying, and made me want to live. I wanted to live for revenge. It didn't matter how long it took, but I was gonna see to it that Junior paid for killing my brother.

As I lay on Ray's bunk thinking about how I could take my revenge out on Junior and listening to my Patti Labelle CDs, I thought I heard a knock at the door. I tiptoed to the front door and peeked out of the peephole. Standing on the other side of the door was Ms. Washington and Officer Crawley.

I opened the door. "Is sumf'n wrong, Ms. Washington?"

"Cameron, Officer Crawley here says that he's been trying to reach your mother, but no one will answer the phone. Is your mother home?"

"Yes, ma'am," I said as they entered the apartment.

Ms. Washington headed towards Mother's bedroom and knocked on her door. "Hello, Janet," she said. "It's Gerdy from next door. Officer Crawley is here, and he would like to speak to you."

"I think she still might be asleep," I said, as I stood in the living room with Officer Crawley. I hoped they would leave.

Ms. Washington opened the door to Mother's bedroom and went in. "Oh my God!" she yelled. "Officer Crawley, please call an ambulance."

Both Officer Crawley and I went into Mother's room and saw Ms. Washington trying to get my mother out of the bed. Mother looked too weak to even stand. Officer Crawley pulled out his walkie-talkie, and speaking in police jargon, demanded a bus be sent to our address.

Officer Crawley led me out of Mother's bedroom and closed the door. "Son, why don't you go out in the living room and wait for the ambulance while we get your mother ready, okay."

I didn't know what they were doing in Mother's bed-room, but in a way, I was hoping that maybe she had died. How dare she not care or love my sister and me enough to wanna live? If she wanted to die, then so be it.

As strange as it sounds, while I waited out in the living room for the ambulance to take Mother to the hospital and possibly save her life, the only person on my mind was Mr. Jamison. With all the anger and hurt I had been feeling, I had suddenly begun to think about sex. It had been a minute since I'd had that "tingling" feeling. I think it's the brain that tries to even things out when your mind and body are going through such emotions. It somehow balances everything out, or helps one's equilibrium, shall I say.

I had to laugh at the thought of feeling a little guilty, because I was so wrapped up into Ray. But then I reminded myself that he was no longer here.

I imagined Mr. Jamison holding me and kissing me and telling me how much he loved me. Suddenly, I snapped out of my embrace with Mr. Jamison because of the loud ambulance siren I heard outside my window.

"Shit!" I said to myself.

The doorbell rang to our apartment. I watched the EMTs carrying medical bags and stretcher exit the ambulance. It was kinda embarrassing as people from the apartments came outside to watch what and who was being carried out.

I pressed the button to allow them to enter the complex, and they ran up the one flight of stairs to my door. They seemed to be in such a hurry as they almost knocked me down as they entered after I opened the door.

"In here, fellas," Officer Crawley announced, as he opened Mother's bedroom door.

I stood out in the living room not knowing what to expect as I waited for them to carry Mother out on the stretcher. *Would they have the sheet over her? Would they have tubes running in and out of her body the same way they had them running in and out of Ray? Would Mother even be alive, or is she dead?*

"Okay, coming through. Watch it, watch it," I heard one of the EMTs say as they carried Mother through the living room and down the hallway steps.

I stood there frozen. I couldn't move as I watched them zoom by with Mother on the stretcher. The covers were not over her head, which told me she wasn't dead, but her facial expression was gaunt-like, and her eyes were rolling around in her head.

My emotions were mixed mainly because, deep down inside, I no longer loved Mother anymore and wanted to be on my own. I just wanted to live my own life without someone telling me what to do, and when, where, and how to do things. At that moment, I wanted to be an adult. I wanted to walk out that door and never come back.

Ms. Washington tried to comfort me with a hug. "Come on, sweetie, you can ride to the hospital with me."

I wanted to scream, "Hell no, I don't wanna go. Just leave me alone!" But no one seemed to care what I thought or how I felt.

*

We finally made it to the hospital and I suddenly felt fear while getting out of Ms. Washington's beat-up 1970 blue-green Buick.

"Cameron, you all right, sweetie?" she asked, coming to my rescue.

"Yes, ma'am, I'm okay." I tried to put on a brave front. Honestly, I was afraid to go inside because this was the same hospital that my brother laid dead in the morgue.

"Come on, sweetie, give me your hand."

I don't know why Ms. Washington felt the need to hold my hand. *I'm not a baby. I'm almost grown. I'm thirteen years old. Hell, I'ma teenager,* I thought to myself.

Anyway, Ms. Washington held my hand as we crossed the street and entered the main lobby of the hospital.

Ms. Washington walked up to the receptionist who sat

behind the Information Desk. "Excuse me," she said. "A good friend of mine was just brought in. Her name is Janet Wilson. Do you know where I might find her?"

The receptionist found Mother's information in her computer. "I see here she's in the emergency room down this hallway." She pointed to our left.

Ms. Washington continued holding my hand as we walked down to the emergency room, where we found a pair of empty seats and sat patiently to hear any news on Mother's condition. My sister Keshia was with one of Ms. Washington's friends, so that left me and Ms. Washington sitting together as I watched her thumb through one magazine after the other. What seemed like hours of waiting was replaced with hunger pangs as I listened and tried to conceal the sounds of my growling stomach.

I wasn't interested in looking through no magazines. Instead I tried to entertain myself by thinking up stories about the people coming into the emergency room complaining of various illnesses.

Then this one black guy came into the waiting room holding his butt and limping. I really didn't know what was wrong with him, but I couldn't help but laugh because in my mind, he got a hold of some dick he couldn't handle.

Ms. Washington leaned over and whispered to me, "It's not nice to laugh at people who aren't feeling well, sweetie."

"I'm sorry," I whispered back, still laughing to myself.

Eventually, Ms. Washington must have become impatient because she told me to wait here as she got up to go speak to one of the doctors at the nurses' desk.

She came back over to me and stated, "You hungry, sweetie? If you are, we can go get something to eat in the cafeteria." She reached out and grabbed my hand.

Minutes later, I was sitting across from Ms. Washington, grubbing down on a loaded bacon cheeseburger and some fries while she just drank a cup of black coffee. Hospital food ain't the best food in the world, but it sure hit the spot.

After feeding my hunger, Ms. Washington and I went back to the emergency room and took our seats, only to continually wait. From time to time, I would sneak and look at her to see if I could read her facial expression, but I couldn't. It looked as though she wanted to tell me something but didn't know how.

"You okay, Ms. Washington?"

"I'm fine, sweetie. Thanks for asking, but I'm the one that need to be asking you. Don't you think?"

"I'm okay. Just sleepy, that's all," I replied, yawning.

"Well, you just come and lay your head down right here on my lap and go to sleep, sweetie."

Ms. Washington was getting on my nerves with that "sweetie" bullshit, but I loved how she truly seemed to care for me and my family. As I lay my head down on her lap, I secretly pretended that she was my real mother as I drifted off to sleep while she stroked the side of my face.

As soon as I dozed off, I heard sounds of someone crying. I tried to focus my eyes on what was going on around me and realized Ms. Washington was the one crying.

I sat up, and there was a doctor sitting across from us, explaining to her that my mom had a nervous breakdown and had to be admitted, and if she didn't respond to treatment, she then would have to be institutionalized. Personally, I wanted to jump for joy.

# Chapter 9

## June 2001

Four years later my dream of having a real mother finally came true. Although, my real mom had to be institutionalized because she could never get over the death of my brother. Ms. Washington had taken me and my sister Keshia in and raised us as her own. Chile, I can't even explain how so many things had changed for the better. My new mom had found true love and actually married a man named William Jenkins about a year ago, and he also adopted me and my sister. So my new name became Cameron Jenkins, and I loved it because now I felt as though I was a part of a real family.

My new dad had a huge colonial-style five-bedroom house in the suburbs, and we moved in with him. And, honies, I had my own bedroom and decorated it with various pictures of models such as Tyra, Iman, and, oh yes, the fabulous Ms. Lena Horne, the diva who started it all. I would sometimes lie across my bed and stare at her picture, wishing she was my real mother.

Don't misunderstand because when Ms. Washington took me and my sister in, I truly felt for the first time in my life, I had a real mother. My new mom would wash our clothes, iron them, and discipline us when we needed it, loved us as though we were her own, and cooked our meals. Every evening at seven p.m. sharp, we all would sit around the dining room table and eat dinner together, like a real family, or at least those I saw on TV.

My favorite TV show was the old reruns of *The Cosby Show*, and I would pretend we were the Huxtable kids. I was Denise Huxtable because I was fierce like that, and my li'l sister was, of course, Rudy. My new dad was the Christian type, a man in his mid-forties who had never been married before and never had any kids of his own. He loved the church and was a deacon, and he made sure that the whole family went to church each and every Sunday. Dad was well liked in the neighborhood by the kids because he owned a small grocery store on the corner and would sometimes give them free candy when they didn't have any money.

Also, much to my surprise, the so-called thugs and wannabe gangsters in the neighborhood had much love and respect for my new dad as well. They would sometimes stop in his store or come by the house just to say hello and talk with him. Dad was very good at giving excellent advice. I loved him because I had become very feminine-acting as I got older, and I knew he knew I was gay, but yet he loved me just the same.

Mom didn't have to work, but she volunteered three days a week down at the hospital. She would help the nurses with some of the older patients, whether it was to help them go to the bathroom or just read a book to them. But she would also make time for me and my sister. For example, she would take an hour or so out of her day just to talk with me to see what was going on in my life, something my real mother had never done. My new mother still called me sweetie, but I couldn't blame her. After all, I was seventeen, better-looking than most girls my age, and had a body built for sex. Or so I was told by some of the boys I had been with.

What I also loved about my new life was, my mom knew

I was gay, and she was cool with it, too. She'd actually sat me down a few months ago and simply asked, "Sweetie, is you gay?"

I didn't know how to respond at first because I didn't know how she would take it, but much to my surprise, she then said, "I know you are because I heard you on the phone the other night talking to some boy."

I knew exactly what she was talking about because I had gotten into an argument with my boyfriend at the time and began to yell at him. So, at that point what else could I say but "Yes, ma'am"? She then kissed me on the forehead and said she still loved me regardless.

Even my li'l sister Keshia, who was now ten years old, knew about my lifestyle.Of course, she didn't know all the gory details, but she knew I liked boys and that I had a new boyfriend. Our relationship got better as well because she didn't go running to our new mom about everything, like she used to with our old mother. My new mom didn't believe in spoiling one child over the other. Thank God.

Tonight Robin and I had our senior prom. My mom and I had been out most of the day trying to find something for me to wear. I didn't want to wear the traditional tuxedo, I wanted to stand out. I bought a pair of black slim-fit jeans, and a pair of black loafers. I was going to wear that with my red chiffon fabric shirt that Robin had made for me. You see, Robin had become an excellent seamstress. Girlfriend could sew her ass off. That's how she made most of her money in school, sewing outfits together for some of the cool girls who had the reputation of being with the in-crowd and being fabulous.

It also didn't hurt that I had helped her to lose those unruly twenty pounds, and with my makeup tips, we thought we were high-fashion models every time we cat-walked the school corridor.

*

Mom yelled through my bedroom door, "Sweetie, Robin on the phone."

73

"Okay, I'll be out in a minute," I yelled back.

After tucking my one-of-a-kind red chiffon shirt down in my jeans and slipping into my loafers, I ran to see what Robin wanted. "Thanks, Ma," I said, taking the phone from her.

While handing me the phone, my mom whispered, "Sweetie, you and Robin are real close. You sure you two aren't involved?"

"No, Ma, that will never happen," I said, my hand over the phone so Ms. Fag-hag couldn't hear.

"Sweetie, you never know what might happen tonight." She winked at me.

"Trust me, Ma. I know."

"Humph. God doesn't know, but my son does."

"Hahahahaha!" Then I said to Robin, "Yeah, Ms. Fag-hag, what's up?"

"What's so funny? Your mom still trying to hook us up again?"

"Mmm-hmm."

"I thought you told her you were gay?"

"Chile boo, she knows. She just tryin' to be funny. So, what's up with you? Why you calling me? You dressed yet?"

"Yeah, I am, but I need you to come over and do my makeup. You didn't forget, did you?"

"Naw, chile. I'll be there in half an hour."

I hung up the phone and went back to my room to add some finishing touches. I stood and looked at my reflection in my floor-length mirror and couldn't get over how cute I was. I had Robin tie in braids to my own hair, which now hung down to my ass. My light-skinned complexion with my dark, thick eyebrows and long eyelashes reminded me of my girl Denise Huxtable. Only, I was much cuter. The red chiffon shirt that Robin made for me had buttoned up on the left side, short sleeves and had a boat collar that showed off my long neck and made my complexion just that much more radiant. I had also gotten my driver's license a few months earlier, and Dad was letting me use his car to drive myself and Robin to the prom.

**74**

About a year or so ago, Robin's family had moved all the way across town, but she'd stayed enrolled at Omaha High. Chile, I couldn't wait for this night to begin, so I could shake my ass.

"Don't go, Cam," my baby sister cried as she stood under my bedroom doorway.

"Aw, what's wrong, Keshia?" I asked, extending my arms out to her.

She fell into my arms. "I don't want you to go to no damn prom."

"Well, why not?"

"I just don't want you to go."

"Why, Keshia?" I looked into her teary eyes. "What's going on with you?"

"If you go, you might not come back either," she replied, holding on to me as tight as she could.

"Either?"

It suddenly dawned on me that she was crying because our brother Ray was gunned down at his prom. To this day, Junior was never punished for what he'd taken from me. I still thought about Ray from time to time and how the hospital turned his body over to the state to bury. Ray had never had a proper funeral, nor did I have a chance to say my final good-byes because the state had cremated his body, and no one seemed to know what happened to the urn he was put into.

Now, the baby sister that used to get on my nerves as a kid was afraid that something would happen to me at my own prom. It had never occurred to me until now the reason why she had been moping around the house for the past couple of days. Ray had always protected me and Keshia, and I loved him for that. I'd never told anyone about the special relationship that he and I had, not even Robin. People can be so uptight about sex. I was yet to find someone who cared for me the way Ray did.

"Keshia, I still miss him too. There's not a day that goes by that I don't think about him, but I'm gonna be all right, okay," I whispered in her ear as I continued to hug her.

"But what if..."

"Shhh! There won't be any *if*. You hear me?"

"Uh-huh."

"And thank you, baby girl."

"Fa-fa-fa what?"

"For loving me and caring about me." I planted a big sloppy kiss on her cheek.

"Aw! I've been kiss by a dog." And just that quick, she pulled away from me, wiping where I had kissed her, and ran to her room.

As I was about to leave, my mom and dad had come out from their bedroom and began making a fuss about how good I looked. Of course, I had to stand and pose while they took pictures, but I didn't mind. Besides, I did look good. Honey, I was the shit, and you couldn't tell me any different.

\*

I pulled up in front of Robin's house still thinking about what Keshia had said. I began to cry as I thought about the last time I had seen Ray. He was lying in the hospital bed with tubes running in and out of his body as though he was just a piece of meat. He didn't even look like himself.

"Uh, excuse you."

I looked up, and there was Ms. Fag-hag standing by my car with her hands on her hips and rolling her neck from side to side.

"Oh, chile boo," I replied, quickly trying to wipe away the tears from my eyes.

"Ms. Thang, why are you just sitting here?"

"Oh, girl, *puh-lease*, don't come for me," I spat, getting out of the car.

"Cam, you look so good. I love that shirt," Robin said, paying herself a compliment. Where did you get it from?"

"What? This old thang?" I replied before we went arm in arm to her house.

After making up Robin's face and posing for pictures that her mom, who I had now began calling Auntie, wanted to take of the two of us.

We finally made it to our prom. We sat in the car smoking a blunt and watched our classmates walk the red carpet with their gowns and tuxedos and enter the gymnasium, where the celebration was being held.

"Oooo, Cam, I'm ready to get my groove on," Robin squealed, as she threw her arms in the air to the sounds of hip-hop blasting from a car that pulled up next to us.

I looked over to see who was in the car, and my mouth fell wide open. I couldn't believe whose face I was staring into. I began to sweat profusely, and nausea quickly set in.

"Chile, what's wrong with you?" Robin asked when she realized I wasn't looking too well.

Practically hyperventilating, I said, "Don't you know who the driver is?"

"No. Should I?"She strained to get a better look at the driver.

"Ms. Thang, stop staring so hard before he notice us," I said, sliding down in my seat.

"Well, how am I gonna know who it is if I don't stare? Humph?" She rolled the window down and leaned outside.

"Girl, would you put that window up and stop it."

"Well, who is it then?" she spat, rolling the window up.

The lump in my throat grew, and the tears began to run down my face. "That's Junior, the bastard that killed Ray."

Robin squealed, "You lying."

"No, I'm not. I would know his ass from a mile away."

"But this guy looks like he's in his late twenties or early thirties. Besides, that was only four years ago, so Junior would be in his mid-twenties by now, and like I said, that guy looks a lot older. So, how can you be sure? And why would he be coming to a senior prom?"

"I don't know, but I know he killed my brother," I replied

confidently, wiping the tears from my eyes.

Robin held my hand to comfort me. "We don't have to go in if you don't want to."

"I should call the dayum po-po on his black ass."

"Why wasn't he locked up anyway? Isn't murder a crime?"

"His ass was locked up initially, but he made bail and the cops hadn't been able to find him since. And you know how the cops are. They ain't that interested in black-on-black crime. Sons of bitches!" I started becoming angry all over again about my brother's murder.

"Look, Cam, I know you're upset, and I feel your pain, sweetie. But tonight is our prom night, and we need to celebrate. Let's call the police and have his ass locked up, so we can enjoy the rest of our evening."

"Naw, sugar, I got other plans for mister man, now that I know he's still here in Omaha."

"What plans, Cam? What plans you got?"

"Never mind, Robin." I started up the car. "Let's just get out of here!"

# Chapter 10

We drove around downtown aimlessly until I remembered hearing about this gay club located in the downtown area. I eventually located the club and parked in front. The club was called "Roscoe's." Neither one of us had ever been inside the club, but I'd heard some crazy stories about the goings-on there. Not to mention the stories I'd read online. Besides, this was my prom night, and even though I didn't wanna go to my prom after seeing Junior there, I still wanted to celebrate and do something different.

"Why you bring me here, Cam?" Robin folded her arms. "You know they not gonna let us in because of our age. Humph!"

"You don't know. We might get lucky, and maybe they'll let us in." I looked at all the children going inside with their fierce outfits on.

"Hey, I saw this movie one time where this young brotha slipped the bouncer some money to let him in the club. Maybe we can do the same thing." Robin looked in her purse and counted all the money she had.

"How much you think we need to pay him?" I asked,

pulling my money outta my pants pocket.

"I don't know. How much do you have?"

"One fifty. You?"

"Almost eighty." Robin gave me all her money.

"That's two hundred thirty dollars. I'm not giving him all this just to get in the club, girl. Hell, I'd suck his dick first before I give him all this." I waved the money in her face, laughing at my own joke.

"Hmm…we'd make out better if you just give him the money, if you ask me."

"Chile boo, you ain't even funny. Let's go," I said, getting out of the car.

We approached the bouncer, a huge white dude that stood about six four, with tattoos going up one side of his arm and down to the other.

"Now, where are you two going?" he asked.

Robin stuttered, "Ah-ah-ah…"

"Oooo, Robin, isn't he a fine specimen of a man?" I rubbed my hand up and down his muscled arm, and trying to flatter this big ol' Olga. "We just tryin'-a have a li'l bit of fun, daddy." I was smiling at him from ear to ear as I slipped him a crisp fifty-dollar bill.

Mr. Bouncer took the money, smiled at me, and held the door open for us as we entered.

"See, bitch? That's how it's done," I said, snapping my fingers.

"You punks sure do stick together, hmm."

"Don't hate, Ms. Thang. You know you love us."

We laughed as we strolled in and walked over to the dance floor.

I didn't know about Robin, but I stood there in awe as I watched men dance with men and women dance with women. This was the first time I had ever seen people just being themselves and having a good time. And even though this was a primarily white club, there were several brothas and sistas scattered amongst the crowd.

Robin yelled over the loud music that was bumping, "I need to go to the bathroom, Cam. Can you come with me?"

"Chile boo, I ain't following you to no bathroom. Don't be scared. Go ahead."

"Humph, fine then."

Robin went through the crowd, searching for the restroom.

With the music pumping, and lights flashing, I was getting sucked right into all the excitement that filled the room. The children were hollering and shouting and moving to the beat. Or at least my brothas and sistas were, considering we're the ones with all the rhythm.

The music sounded so good to my ears, I couldn't help but join in on the fun. I started dancing right where I stood.

Voguing from one side of the room to the other, I suddenly stood in my tracks when I noticed this fine brotha on the other side of the dance floor, just standing there, drinking his beer.

Wow! Was it who I really thought it was? *Naw, it can't be,* I thought.

"Thanks for nothing, punk," Robin shouted in my ear.

"Oh, girl, please, get over it." I yelled back, still staring at the brotha.

"Ms. Thang." Robin hit me on my shoulder. "Who you staring at?"

"You see that brotha over there with the wifebeater on and jeans, drinking his beer?"

"Oh my God! That ain't who I think it is, is it?"She again hit me on the shoulder.

"Bitch, if you hit me one more time." I turned around and faced her, my hands on my hips.

"Oh, stop being a baby," she scuffed, waving her hand at me. "But, for real though, is that who I think it is?"

"Mr. Jamison is the flesh."

Robin squealed, "Oooo, I knew he was gay. I just knew it. Especially when he started teaching gym."

"Oh, girl, hush. You didn't know nothing."

"So."

"So what?"

"Aren't you going over and speak to him?"

"Chile, I don't know. What am I supposed to say?"

"Say hello, silly."

"And then what?"

"Oooo, you better think of something quick because he must have noticed you staring at him. And he's on his way over here. Bye!" she said, walking away.

"Robin, come back here." I turned to grab her arm, but it was too late. She had already disappeared into the crowd.

"Hey, little man. How you doing this evening?" I heard him ask.

"I-I-I-I'm good." I almost tripped over my own feet as I turned around.

"Whoa! You okay?"

"Yeah, I am. Sorry about that. I think maybe I've had a little too much to drink," I said, lying through my teeth.

"Oh, I see. You know, I might be wrong, but I noticed you when you first walked in, and I haven't seen you drink anything as of yet. Am I wrong?"

I don't know what it was about this man, but he still made me weak in the knees. And, honey, I hadn't seen this man in over three years, and I was getting goose bumps.

"Hello? Am I wrong?"

"I'm sorry. No, you're not wrong." I stared into his beautiful bedroom eyes.

"I'm Keith, by the way," he stated as he extended his hand to shake mine.

I shook his hand in return. "I'm Cam." I realized he didn't have a clue as to who I was.

"It's nice to meet you, Cam. Ah, you're kinda young. You mind if I ask how old you are?"

I answered with a slight attitude, "I'm twenty-two. How old are you?"

"I'm thirty-two." He looked as though he didn't believe me, taking a closer look at my facial features.

"What's wrong? Do I have something on my face or something?"

"Yeah, you do, as a matter of fact."

"And what's that?" I brushed the braids out of my face, trying to look grown up.

"Youth and familiarity," he said with a smile.

"What is that supposed to mean?" I said, folding my arms.

"Hey, let's go over on the other side where we can sit down and talk, where it's not so loud. You game?"He held his hand out, allowing me to lead the way.

I didn't know where I was going, but I followed the crowd going in the direction Robin and I had entered. I looked for her as I continued to walk and noticed that she was on the dance floor dancing with some sissy. *She's such a fag-hag*, I thought to myself. I gave her a thumbs-up to let her know I was okay, and she returned the gesture.

We made our way over to the other side of the club, where it was more secluded and less noisy.

"Would you like something to drink?" Mr. Jamison asked, before taking a seat at a booth.

"Ah, I'll have whatever you're having," I replied, not really knowing what to ask for.

"Okay, I'll be right back."

I sat there thinking how sexy Mr. Jamison looked in his wifebeater and loose-fitting jeans that hung off his firm melon-shaped booty. Chile, I was so moist between my legs. I couldn't believe that I was actually spending time with a man that I had dreamed about so many times in my past.

It's interesting how, once you stop thinking about someone, they seem to pop up out of nowhere. Just like I had stopped thinking about Junior, and out of nowhere, he showed up at my prom. Now, here I sat spending time with Mr. Jamison. Ain't that a trip? And, honey, I was gonna enjoy every minute of it.

I remembered that day back in gym class when he was showing us how to swim and he grabbed me around my waist to keep me from drowning. My little fourteen-year-old body rubbed up against his hard manly body, and I thought I was gonna faint. Be still, my racing heart. Then, suddenly, it dawned on me that Mr. Jamison didn't even remember who I was. And, for some reason, that saddened me.

"I hope I wasn't gone too long, Cam." Mr. Jamison handed me a Corona with a slice of lime on top.

"Naw, not at all." I took a sip of my Corona, still trying to act grown up.

"That's good because you are way too sexy-looking to be left alone too long, and I didn't want to have to fight somebody to get them away from you." Keith looked at me as though he could eat me alive.

"Wow!" I turned to face him. "Keith, that was really nice of you to say, but you don't even remember who I am. Why is that?"

"Who said I didn't remember you?" he said, looking dead in my eyes.

"So who am I?"

"You're Cameron Wilson, from my seventh-grade math class a few years ago. And I know you can't be no older than eighteen. So, how did you get in here?" he asked with a raised eyebrow.

I was so shocked that he remembered who I was, my mouth practically dropped to the floor. I felt so stupid, trying to act so grown up, and he knew all along I was just putting on a show. Something inside of me just wanted to get up and leave, but another side of me wanted him to hold me tight and kiss me like I'd never been kissed before.

Out of nowhere, I asked, "Can I kiss you?" Before he had a chance to answer, I literarily threw myself at him and kissed him dead in the mouth.

"Whoa!" he said, pulling away. "Cameron, slow yo' roll, shawty."

**84**

"I-I-I-I'm sorry, Mr. Jamison…I mean Keith. I've just always wanted to do that since the day I walked into your classroom," I answered softly, ashamed at being rejected.

In the back of my mind though, all I could think about was how juicy his lips were.God had answered prayer, because Mr. Jamison was beautiful.

"I'm flattered, Cameron, I really am, but you're a little too young for me. Don't get me wrong, you've grown into a very attractive shawty, but I'm not into minors."

"But I'll be eighteen in a few months," I whined.

"I tell you what, here's my card.Give me a call if you ever just want to talk or need help getting into a good university." Keith handed me his card and walked away.

After getting my thoughts together and figuring out how I was gonna make Mr. Jamison my man, I went to the other side of the club to check on my girl Robin. And, just as I thought, she was surrounded by so many queens, and the music was so loud, I couldn't get her attention to let her know I was ready to leave.

I stood around the dance floor and noticed Mr. Jamison bumping and grinding with some little white queen. Chile, no, that bitch wasn't gonna take my man. I became so furious, I strutted right out on the dance floor and got in between Mr. Jamison and her. So, as I did the bump and grind with Mr. Jamison, he didn't seem to care what was going on, because he was so into the music and obviously had a little too much to drink, that he continued to bump and grind along with me.

Fortunately, Ms. Thang got the message and stomped off the dance floor. This was fine by me because Mr. Jamison and I danced like we were the only two on the dance floor.

His manhood was so big and hard as I felt it pressed against my crotch while we continued to bump and grind to the music, I thought I was in heaven. Mr. Jamison held on to my small waist, looked me in my eyes, and licked his lips like LL Cool J. Honey, that was all it took.

I leaned in and kissed him once again. And this time, he suddenly stopped dancing and pulled my face away from his with the palm of his hands. He looked at me strangely at first and then said something that I didn't hear because the music was so loud. He then pulled me into him and kissed me so passionately that, in my mind, everything froze in time…the music, the flashing lights, people on the dance floor, and more importantly, my heart.

Our moment in time came to an end when the club lights began to flash on and off and the DJ announced, "Last call."

"Ah dayuuuum, shawwwwty! I didn't mean to do dat," Mr. Jamison slurred. He pulled away from me and began stumbling off the dance floor.

I wanted to run after him and beg him to be with me, but that would've made me look like a desperate, immature, little queen. I thought the best thing for me to do was to wait a few days, call him and let him know I needed some serious help.

"Chile, that man don't know what he's in for," I said to myself, searching the crowd for Ms. Fag-hag.

Moments later, I saw Robin outside talking to a group of queens standing in the parking lot. "Robin, are you ready to go?" I asked, as I stood in front of her and her new friends.

"Heeeey, Cam, le-le-let me in-introduce you to my friends."

"Chile boo, your ass is drunk." I grabbed her by the waist. "I'm gonna take you home so you can sleep that shit off."

"Bye, y'all. I-I guess it-it time ta-ta go, huh."

"Yes, it is, my lil fag-hag," I replied, walking her to the car.

By the time we got on the highway, Ms. Fag-hag was out like a light. I turned on the radio to keep me company. I thought about Mr. Jamison taking me in his arms and passionately kissing me. Be still, my nerves. Lawd have mercy, Jesus. I was determined to have that man if that was the last thing I did.

I pulled up in front of Robin's house thirty or so minutes later and parked. I helped her out of the car, but she was still half-'sleep and drunk as a skunk, as Mother would say. Fortunately, her mom was peeking out the window as we got to the door.

Auntie opened the door. "Cam, what's wrong with my baby? Is she all right?"

"She's okay, Auntie. Just had one too many to drink," I replied, helping Robin inside.

"For heaven sakes, Cam, why you let her drink so much? You know you're not supposed to drink and drive, baby." Auntie started to help me take Robin upstairs to her bedroom.

"Auntie, calm down. I wasn't drinking, just Robin."

She looked up at the ceiling."Lawd, what am I gonna do with this chile?"

"Auntie, Robin will be fine. Just let her sleep it off."

*

By the time I made it home, it was a little after three a.m. As I pulled up into the driveway, all the lights were out, except for a dim light coming from the basement.

I entered thinking, maybe I should get my dad to come check and see what was going on in the basement, but then if it was nothing, he might be upset because I had awakened him. Especially since he had to be at work and open up his store by seven a.m.

I crept into the kitchen and grabbed one of Mom's big ol' wooden cooking spoons, tiptoed to the basement door, and quietly turned the doorknob and cracked the door open. I stood at the top of the stairs to see if I could hear any noise, but all I could make out was mumbling sounds.

I eased down the stairs, taking one step at a time. Even though I couldn't see what was happening, I could hear what was being said.

"Ah, suck that dick like you want it, old man," a voice whispered.

*Old man? What the fuck?* The closer I got to the bottom of the stairs, I realized the slurping sounds, and moaning and groaning were coming from the back of the basement.

**87**

I tiptoed around the staircase and stood in the entrance before going into the back part of the basement, and honey, what I saw almost made me throw up. My new daddy was on his knees, sucking this guy's dick. Chile, I didn't know what to do. I stood there practically in shock, trying to make out who the guy was, but I couldn't. The guy was sitting in a chair with his back towards me, but I could see my new daddy as clear as day, bobbing his head up and down, gagging on this dude's dick.

"Come on, old man, suck J.R.'s dick like you mean it," the guy said, breathing heavily.

I couldn't make out the voice, but just as I was about to tiptoe back upstairs, I turned around and hit my pinky toe on the leg of a chair that Momma had sitting right by the entrance. "Ouch, shit!" I grabbed my foot.

I heard my stepfather say, "Who's that?"

Chile, at that point, I took off hobbling upstairs as fast as I could. I jumped in my bed and pulled the covers over me as though I had been asleep, just in case my daddy came in.

Within minutes, he opened my door. "Cameron," he whispered.

I lay perfectly still as my pinky toe continued to throb.

He came in and sat on the side of my bed.

*Oh shit!*

"Cameron, I know it was you, so stop playing possum," he said in a whisper.

Again, I said nothing.

"Look, faggot, if you keep acting like you're 'sleep, I will beat your ass," he said angrily.

"Yes, sir," I responded, like a little kid.

"If you repeat any of what you just saw to anybody, I will kill you and your sister."

With that, he rose from my bed and made his exit, leaving me to wonder, *What the fuck is going on here?* Baby, I was so scared, I didn't know what to do.

# Chapter 11

Since that night, I stayed as far away as possible from my stepfather. Monday through Saturday, he worked at the store from seven a.m. to eleven p.m., and on Sundays, the family stayed in church most of the day, for morning and evening services.

I used to go to church with my family and stay there most of the day as well, but after that night, I lost all respect for my dad, especially since he was one of the head deacons at our church. Of course, it didn't have anything to do with him being gay or bisexual, or whatever you wanna call it. It was because he was married to my mom, and I thought he loved only her. But I guess I was wrong.

My girl Robin and I had graduated from high school about a week ago, and while she studied to take her SAT and apply to different universities, I just moped around the house, feeling sorry for myself, but mostly for my mom. I hadn't told her what I saw or what my stepfather had said to me. I felt bad for her because I knew how much she loved him.

Over the summer, my little sister had been staying over one of her friends' house, and my mom was spending more time volunteering her services at the hospital. Which left me in the house by myself most of the day. Several times, I picked up the phone to call Mr. Jamison, but chickened out at the last minute and hung up. I didn't know what to say to him. I didn't wanna tell him what I saw because I was afraid it might get out some kinda way and get back to my dad, and he'd carry out his threat.

As I sat on my bed, listening to my Patti Labelle CDs and staring at the divas posted on my walls, I realized I hadn't eaten much of anything within the past couple of weeks, and my stomach was making it known, loud and clear. I went downstairs to the kitchen to check out what was in the icebox, but there really wasn't anything in there I had a taste for. I went back to my room and threw on one of my torn T-shirts and a pair of sweats, grabbed my keys, and decided to go to the local market and make a fresh salad.

\*

I parked in the grocery store parking lot. As I was about to get out of my car, I saw Junior once again. This time, he was standing in the middle of the parking lot with several other brothas, talking and laughing, his car stereo system blasting.

At first, I thought about not getting out and just pulling off, but then I thought, *This muthafucka probably don't even remember who I am.* So, I got out of my car and acted as though I didn't even notice him.

As I walked by, one of the brothas tried to be funny and, in a high-pitched voice, said, "Heeey, sunshine."

I continued walking with my head hung low without saying a word because regardless of whatever I said, they would've only ignored it and tried to punk me out anyway. I made my way in the grocery store with a cart and went from aisle to aisle, stalling for time, hoping that by the time I left out, they would be gone.

After thirty or so minutes, I purchased all the ingredients I needed to make a fabulous chef's salad. As I gathered my bag and exited the grocery store, I noticed the guys had left, but sitting on the hood of my car was Junior.

"What's yo' name?" he asked as I approached the driver's side of my car.

"Who wants to know?" I asked, being somewhat sarcastic.

"I'm Junior," he replied, getting off the hood of my car and extending his hand to shake mine.

"I'm Sunshine." I left his handshake hanging while I put my groceries in the backseat.

"Well, I normally don't do this, Sunshine, because I'm definitely a ladies' man." He leaned over and whispered in my ear, "But you look good to me for some reason."

"So, what do you want?" I questioned angrily, getting in my car.

"Dayum, Sunshine! Why you being so mean?" He got into the passenger side.

"Look, Junior, or whatever your name is, I have some place to be, so I would appreciate if you would get out." I started up my car.

"Okay, cool. I understand if you got another nigga, but check this." He went into his baggy jean pocket and pulled out a wad of money. He then placed five crisp hundred-dollar bills on the dashboard. "Get something nice to wear tonight because we're going out."

"Excuse you?"

"Give me your number."

"For what?"

"So I can call and pick you up at seven p.m. sharp."

"I'm not giving…"

"I said, give me your number," he replied in an angry tone.

I don't know why, but I blurted out my number, hoping he would at least get out of my car. Fortunately, he placed my number in his cell and left.

I grabbed the money from my dashboard and just stared at it. Was this Negro serious? Was he seriously expecting me to go buy a five-hundred-dollar outfit, like some hoochie, just to take me out? *And his stupid ass don't even remember who I am.*

Paying his black ass back for killing my brother was gonna be easier than I thought.

*

By the time I finished stuffing my face and watching back-to-back episodes of *America's Next Top Model*, I finally dozed off to sleep. But as soon as I got into a deep sleep, my ringing cell phone woke me up.

"Hello," I said, trying to wake myself up.

"Hey, Sunshine. You ready?"

I sat up in the bed. "Who is this?"

"This is Junior. You ready?"

"What time is it?"

"It's seven p.m., Sunshine. Give me your address so I can pick you up."

"Ah, why don't I just meet you somewhere, because my folks really don't like people coming to our house." I didn't want this murderer to know where I lived.

"Dayum, Sunshine! But that's cool. You know where the Radisson Hotel is downtown, right?"

"Yeah."

"Be there in thirty minutes. Go to the front desk and tell them you are Sunshine. There will be an envelope waiting for you. Bye."

"Hello, hello." I looked at the phone. "No, he didn't just hang up the dayum phone in my ear. Chile, this muthafucka here…Oooo, no, he didn't."

I looked at my phone to check the time and it said 7:11 p.m. I jumped out of bed, took a quick shower, and put some clothes on. I really didn't care how I looked, but I was curious about what he had planned.

*

Honey, I finally made it down to the hotel, parked my car

in the hotel garage, and approached the front desk.

"Ah, yes, my name is Sunshine. I believe you have an envelope for me," I said to the old gray-haired female clerk.

She looked at me as though she smelled something funny.

"Ms. Thang, is there a problem?"

"No, I'm sorry. Please forgive me. Here is your envelope, ma'am…I mean sir."

"It's *sir, biotch.*" I snatched the envelope and walked into the lobby area to read what was inside.

**Dear Sunshine,**

**I'm glad you came. Enclosed is a key to room 4225, I hope you will use it.**

**Junior**

**P.S. I have a surprise for you**

Well, I have to admit, that was very nice of him to arrange all of this. I mean, really, no one had ever done this kinda thing for me before.

*Junior has a little class, I see,* I thought as I caught the elevator to the forty-second floor.

I thought about calling Robin and telling her what Junior had done, getting us a room at the Radisson, but I realized she would probably talk me out of it, saying shit like, "All he wanna do is fuck you. Why would you let him do that after what he did to your brother?"

Yeah, yeah, yeah, I know. But for the past several weeks, I'd been somewhat sad and depressed. And who could blame me? Especially after witnessing what my dad was doing behind my mom's back, I didn't know what to do. My dad's words that night, "I will kill you and your sister," still haunt me to this day.

I found Room 4225, placed the card in the slot, and the door opened. I walked in, and the room was fabulous. Junior must have ordered dinner because there were silver serving trays placed on the dining room table with candles lit on both sides. And he had rose petals scattered throughout the room, leading up to this large king-size bed. I was so surprised that Junior had done all this just for me, I found myself liking him just a little bit more. My eighteenth birthday was in a few days, and in my mind, this was a celebration, just for that occasion.

I walked over to the table and noticed that Junior had poured two flute glasses of champagne. I stood there sipping on it, feeling like the diva I wanted to be and wondering where Junior was.

I was beginning to feel a little bad because Junior had gone through all this trouble, and I didn't even bother to dress up for the occasion, even though he gave me five hundred dollars to get a new outfit. I stood in front of large mirror on the left-hand side of the wall to try to fix myself up a little. But to be honest, I didn't look that bad in my slim fitted jeans, my one–of-a-kind purple T-shirt with rhinestones that Robin had made for me, and a pair of purple sneakers with rhinestones that I had tacked on the front of each shoe. I still had the extensions that Robin had put in my hair, and they were holding up quite well.

I reached in my handbag for a rubber band to at least pull my braids back into a ponytail. I also pulled out my compact just to add a little foundation to my face because I was looking a little pale.

"There, that's better," I said out loud.

Junior walked into the room, catching me off guard. "I'm glad you came."

"Oh, hey."

"So, what do you think, Sunshine?" he asked, arms stretched out wide, referring to the room.

"It's fabulous."

"Are you hungry?"

He pulled the chair out from the table for me to sit, and I sat down at the table.

"A little."

For the next forty-five minutes or so, Junior and I ate and talked about everything under the sun. I found out that today was his twenty-fourth birthday, and he wanted to spend it with me.

Which really touched me. Be still, my beating heart.

He also told me that he had been selling and dealing in drugs ever since he was twelve years old. Junior also told me that he had a girlfriend and a three-and-a-half-year-old daughter named Brianna. But, most importantly, he wasn't gay, but enjoyed having his dick sucked and fucking dudes from time to time.

I didn't really say too much to Junior about myself because I know how much guys like talking about themselves. And the less said about me, the better.

We had finished eating, and Junior invited me to have a seat on the couch with him. Chile, I have to confess, he did look pretty good with his white Calvin Klein sweat suit on, his silver chain with crossbones medallion hanging, and his new white Air Force Ones. He'd obviously been working out because his toned physique was apparent in his all-white attire.

Junior made himself comfortable on the couch. "So, Sunshine, did you enjoy the food?"

"Yes, I did," I replied, sitting next to him.

"Well, tell me more about you."He looked me dead in the eye.

"What do you wanna know?"

"What's your real name?"He got up and grabbed the champagne bottle and glasses we'd left on the dining room table.

"You've been calling me Sunshine, so you can continue to call me that," I cooed, batting my eyes at him.

"But I wanna know your real name." He poured us some more champagne.

"My name is Sunshine, sweetie. That's all you really need to know, right?"

He handed me my glass of champagne. "Is that right?"

The next thing I knew, Junior took the champagne bottle and bashed it up against my head. He hit me so hard, the bottle broke, and I fell off the couch onto the floor. My head was pounding so bad, I knew something in my head must have cracked.

I tried reaching for the couch to pull myself up, but he grabbed me by my shirt, pulled me up off the floor, and with all his might, punched me dead in my right eye. The pain was so excruciating, I couldn't even scream.

All I could hear was Junior yelling, "You seriously didn't think I knew who your faggot ass was? Are you fuckin' kidding me? You think you were going to get away with that shit? Do you know who the fuck I am?"

He continued punching me, throwing my body from one side of the room to the other, sending pictures crashing down from the walls, and lamps from end tables. He then grabbed me by my ponytail and swung me so hard on top of the dining room table, it broke in half. I was in so much pain, I thought I was dying.

I lay there bleeding and crying and begging him to stop, but he didn't.

He picked me up off the floor and tore my bloody clothes off and threw me up against the wall so hard where the mirror hung, it cracked. I could feel the glass cutting into my back.

He then grabbed me by my neck, stared me right in the eye. "You're that punk-ass Cameron, Ray's little brother, and I'ma kill you just like I killed him. But, first, let me give you your surprise."

He threw me back on the floor, held my head against the plush carpet, and spread my legs apart as he entered me from behind. My insides felt as though they were being ripped apart as I continued crying and wiping the blood trickling down my face.

He then propped me up on my knees and began fucking me doggy-style. All I could do was pray to God for His mercy because I knew this was it. I could actually feel my body shutting down.

"Yo, Kurt and Rodney, y'all want to hit some of this ass?"

Barely conscious, I wasn't sure who Junior was talking to, but I tried to raise my head up off the floor. I couldn't make out who the other two guys were coming out of the bathroom in my direction.

Junior was obviously done with me because he asked his boys, "Who wanna go next?"

I tried closing my eyes, hoping I would just pass out, but both of my eyes hurt to the point where I eventually lost my sight completely.

Someone then turned me on my back, and I started to feel warm liquid glazing my body. The liquid stung as it hit every cut and scratch I'd received, and because of the smell, I knew they all were taking turns peeing on me. Not only were they abusing me physically, but mentally as well.

I knew God hated me for what I had done with Ray. Now, I knew for sure. I don't know if the other guys raped me or not, because my body had lost all nerve endings. And, to be honest, I really didn't care one way or the other. I just wanted to die.

And then my wish came true, because everything went black.

*

My eyes were so swollen when I returned from death, I couldn't see anything. I tried to get up, but every bone in my body was crying out to be healed. I tried to open my mouth to yell for help, but I could hardly speak. I lay there feeling around for my handbag, hoping to get my cell phone, so I could call my mom. Even though I couldn't speak that loudly or clearly, she would somehow know I was in trouble.

Oh God, the pain pulsated through every limb of my body.

I began to smell a bad odor. It smelled like burning blood, and worse yet, it seemed to be coming from inside of me. I don't know whether Junior had drugged me or not, but I was scared and wanted to contact somebody, anybody.

But, again, everything went black.

# $\mathcal{C}$hapter 12

I had awakened again and still couldn't see, but this time I was lying in a bed. I tried to feel my face and felt bandages around my eyes and head, and tubes running in and out of my nose. My body still ached like hell, but I wanted to know where I was and if I was safe?

"Is anybody there?" I asked in a hoarse voice.

"Oh praise God! Cam, baby, how you feeling?" I heard my mom ask, as she placed her hands in mine.

I was so happy to hear her voice, I started crying because I didn't think I would ever see her again.

"Ma," I replied, straining my voice as it cracked.

"Yes, sweetie, I'm here."

I squeezed her hands. "Ma, it hurts."

"I know, baby, I know. The doctors gave you some pain medicine, so try to lie still. God will take away the pain, if you pray."

I wanted to scream and let her know that God was the one that allowed this to happen in the first place and He didn't give a shit about me, one way or the other. Instead, I said nothing as my mom sat on the side of the bed and held me in her arms. I cried like a baby while she rocked me back to sleep.

*

A few days had passed, and even though I spent my eighteenth birthday lying in this hospital bed, I was beginning to feel a lot better. My mom, my baby sister, Robin, and even my dad had come by, brought presents, flowers, and they sang and wished me a happy birthday.

I really enjoyed seeing my girl Robin, until she wanted to get all the dirt, as she put it, to know what happened and who did it. I told her the same thing I told the police when they came wanting to know what had happened. I gave bits and pieces but didn't tell them that Junior did it. One, I didn't want Junior to come looking for me, and two, payback is a bitch. Trust me, I had plans for Junior, but until then, I decided to be a good little queen and do what the doctors told me so I could get back to normal.

"Good morning, Cameron. How are you, today?" Beth asked. She was my morning nurse.

I yawned. "I'm feeling better."

"That's always good to hear." She started taking my vitals. "Wow! I see all the flowers and presents. Did my favorite patient have a birthday?"

"Yeah, my birthday was yesterday."

"Awwww! Well, happy belated birthday." Beth wrote some notes on her clipboard.

"Thank you."

"Looks like somebody will be going home in a day or two, huh?"

I smiled. "So they tell me."

"Well, just take it easy, and good luck," Beth said, leaving my room.

I lay in bed most of the morning just watching TV. My mom would stop in periodically to check on me. I was glad they'd brought me to the hospital where my mom volunteered because I would get to see her four or five times throughout the

**100**

day. Robin would stop by from time to time as well, but again, she was busy studying for her SAT.

Today, for some reason, I was feeling somewhat anxious, and I didn't know why. I got up from my bed, went to the bathroom, and decided to walk around the hospital floor I was on. I felt like an old man walking around in my hospital robe and rolling this IV contraption hooked up to my arm. Every room I walked by, people's injuries or sickness seemed to become worse and worse.

After thirty minutes or so, this hospital was beginning to depress me, so I decided to go back to my room. As soon as I was about to enter, I was taken by surprise because there was a guy standing with his back to the door, looking at all of the cards and presents I had sitting in the windowsill.

"Excuse you," I said, standing at the entrance of my room.

Mr. Jamison turned around and faced me. "Hey. How are you doing?"

"What are you doing here?" I asked.

"Does that mean you're sorry I came?"

"No, I mean, how did you know I was here?" I responded, trying to get into bed.

"I ran into your friend Robin. I believe that's what she said her name was. She told me what happened and that you were here."He tried to help me get in bed. "And I just wanted to make sure you were okay."

"Oh really? Why is that?"

He sat on the bed next to me. "Look, I think you're a cool little brotha, and I do like you. So, is that a crime?"

"Like me? Like me how?" I asked, surprised by his confession.

"See, now you playing with me. You know what I meant when I said I liked you."He flashed his Colgate smile at me.

Chile, my depression, pain, and everything else went out of the window. I found myself getting that tingly feeling, the same feeling I felt ever since I'd laid eyes on him.

Mr. Jamison and I talked for hours. He told me about how and why he became a school teacher. He then started teasing me about the time I was in his gym class when he was teaching the boys how to swim and I pretended to be drowning. He said he felt my erection against his outer thigh when he dived in the water to save me. Even though I was a little embarrassed, I had to laugh along with him.

After the laughter, a nervous silence filled the room. Mr. Jamison looked at me as though his eyes wanted to know what had truly happened to me.

I began to pour out my heart. I don't know why, but I told him every gory detail, more than I'd even told my mom or the police, and just reliving it brought tears to my eyes.

When I finished, he held my hand and said, "I'm so sorry that happened to you. I wish I could take it back or erase it from your memory, but I can't. All I can do is be there for you and see you through it."

I didn't understand what Mr. Jamison was saying. He was talking like he had something to do with this, but this had nothing to do with him. I just assumed that this was his way of comforting me. He then said something that really overwhelmed me.

"Cameron, if you ever need to just get away…I live alone and you can come and stay with me."

"Really?" I asked, excited.

"Absolutely. Whenever you like." He showed that Colgate smile once again. "But…"

"See, I knew you didn't mean it."

"Oh, but I did."

"So, why did you say *but*?"

"You have to be legal. You have to wait until you're eighteen."

"Yesterday was my birthday. I just turned eighteen, see," I said like a little kid, pointing to all the birthday cards that sat in the windowsill.

Mr. Jamison looked over at my birthday cards. "So you

are. How could I have forgotten that quickly?"

Mr. Jamison and I talked and joked for another hour or so but were interrupted when my mom came in the room.

"Hey, sweetie. How are you feeling today?" Mom asked, looking strangely at Mr. Jamison.

"I'm feeling good, Ma. By the way, this Mr. Jamison. Mr. Jamison, this is my mom."

Mr. Jamison stood up and shook my mom's hand. "It's nice to meet you, ma'am."

"You too," my mom said, returning the gesture.

Mr. Jamison said, "Well, Cam, I guess I've taken up enough of your time. Call me when you get home, okay."

"Okay, I will," I replied like some lovesick puppy.

\*

My first week at home was fabulous. My mom waited on me hand and foot. My little sister Keshia even pitched in and helped Mom around the house with the cleaning, bringing me my food in bed and washing the dishes.

Robin was still busy with her SAT, but we spoke every night before going to bed. I told her that Mr. Jamison had stopped by the hospital to see me and had even invited me to come and stay with him. Ms. Fag-hag was floored.

Ms. Fag-hag started telling me about Kurt, her new boyfriend. His name sounded familiar, but I couldn't remember where I had heard it. But she went on and on about how sexy he was and how he gave her money just to go shopping. I was genuinely happy for Robin. She was good people, and she deserved to be happy.

As for my stepdad, we only spoke in passing.

A few weeks later, I caught my stepdad several times giving head to these little boys in the neighborhood. This one little boy who went by the name Crisco, I knew for a fact, was only fifteen.

And the following day, Crisco's friend Damien, who was only sixteen, had stopped by, and my stepdad serviced him too.

My stepdad didn't know I saw him, because he thought I was still bedridden, but I wasn't.

What my stepdad was doing made me angry and physically sick. Yet still, he walked around here and went to church every Sunday like nothing ever happened. I could never forgive him for what he was doing and what he'd said to me. And again, the only reason why I'd never mentioned it to my mom was because I knew it would hurt her deeply and I couldn't bring myself to be the cause of that pain.

The police had stopped by a couple of times. The first time was to get my story again, and the second time was to bring some mugs shots, hoping I would be able to pick out the thugs who did this to me. Of course, my story never wavered, and even though I saw Junior's picture in the mix, I never pointed him out. I had other plans for Junior.

This one day, when I thought I was home alone, I had come down the stairs to fix me something to eat.

Before walking into the kitchen, I heard a familiar voice say, "Who's yo' daddy?"

I stopped in my tracks, tiptoed, and hid behind the dining room door. I peeked in, and my mouth almost hit the floor. My stepdad was leaning up against the kitchen table, and Junior was fucking him. I couldn't believe it. I became dizzy and thought I was going to faint, so I grabbed one of the dining room chairs just to hold myself up.

I tiptoed back upstairs to my room and closed my bedroom door. I lay down on my bed in the fetal position with the covers over my head and rocked myself back and forth. The idea of Junior being in my house terrified me. All I wanted to do was get the hell out of here.

I peeked out of the covers and grabbed my cell phone and called Robin to see if she was home, but she wasn't. My mom was at the hospital, doing her volunteer work.

*Think, chile, think*, I thought to myself. And then it dawned on me. *Mr. Jamison.* He'd told me to call him when I got home anyway.

**104**

"What did I do with his card?" I asked myself. I got out of my bed and pulled every piece of clothing in my closet out on the floor.

After several minutes of searching and throwing my clothes about my room like a mad person, I finally came across Mr. Jamison's card. I climbed back in my bed, threw the covers over my head, and dialed the number on the card.

"Hello," Mr. Jamison said.

I whispered, "Ah, Mr. Jamison, this is Cameron. Can you come get me?"

"Who is this again?"

"This is Cameron."

"Cameron, what's wrong? Why are you whispering? I can barely hear you."

"Somebody is here in my house, and I don't wanna be here. Can you come get me?" I asked, practically begging.

"Sure, no problem. Where are you?"

"Can you meet me on the corner of Centre Street and Malcolm Avenue in twenty minutes?"

"See you then," he said, and hung up the phone.

I got fully dressed in no time.

As soon as I opened my door, my stepdad was at the top of the stairs. He turned towards me and asked, "Where are you going?"

Chile, I was so scared, I felt like Ms. Celie in *The Color Purple*. And like Ms. Celie, the only thing that came to my mind was, "Nowhere!" My heart was about to jump out of my chest.

My stepdad walked into his bedroom, so I closed the door and placed my hand across my chest. "Whew, chile! Be still, my heart," I said, breathing heavily, leaning up against the door. *That was too close for comfort*, I thought to myself.

I looked at my watch and realized I only had six minutes or so to meet Mr. Jamison. The location I'd given him was a few blocks away. I tiptoed over to one of my bedroom windows and pulled it up as far as it would go. I climbed out onto the roof and looked over the edge to see how far I would have to jump. Baby, there was no way I could jump from there without spraining something.

I started to go back inside my bedroom window, but then I heard someone knocking on my bedroom door. I turned around, walked back over to the edge of the roof, counted to ten, and jumped.

Fortunately, I only got stuck by some thorns from the bushes outside my house. I got up, brushed myself off, and walked as fast as my little yella ass would take me.

I reached the corner where I told Mr. Jamison to meet me, and sure enough, I saw him sitting there in his black 2001 Escalade. He must have been jamming to the music because he was bobbing his head up and down and didn't notice me standing there.

I knocked on the passenger side window to get his attention.

"Hey, shawty," he said, opening the door for me and turning down his rap music.

"Hey, yourself." I climbed in and buckled my seat belt.

"What's going on?" he asked, pulling away from the curb. "What was the emergency?"

"I'm never going back to that house again."

"What happened?" He looked over at me. I guess he realized I really didn't want to talk about it.

"Look, why don't I take you to my house. You can freshen up, get a good meal, and relax. How's that? Would you like that?"

"Yes, I would love that."

# Chapter 13

We drove on the outskirts of town into a very exclusive neighborhood. I'd been in this area only one time in my life, when my mom had taken a job house-sitting for this old, rich white lady. I started thinking, *How could Mr. Jamison afford living here on a teacher's salary?*

We pulled up in front of a black wrought iron gate that appeared to wrap around acres of property. Mr. Jamison punched in a few numbers, and the gate opened automatically. We drove along a brick road with manicured bush on both sides, and a whole lot of lawn to go with it. I didn't know how many acres of land this property held, but I was in awe. Mr. Jamison knew I was impressed because he kept looking at me out the corner of his eyes and smiling.

As I looked ahead, we were approaching what looked like a mansion. "Whose place is this?" I asked.

We came to a stop at the front door.

"Mine," he said in a matter-of-fact tone. "Come on, let's go."

I opened the car door and walked behind him. I couldn't wait to see what it looked like on the inside. *Honey, Robin gonna gag when she sees where a true diva s'pose to live,* I thought to myself.

Mr. Jamison opened the door and allowed me to enter first. I walked in and stood in the middle of the foyer with my mouth hung open in complete awe. The wooden floors were bare and so shiny, I could actually see my reflection in them.

"What's wrong? Are you okay?" Mr. Jamison walked past me, into the sunken living room area.

"I'm fine," I replied, trying not to seem too pressed. But the truth of the matter was, I was pressed. Very pressed. I had never seen a place like this other than on *MTV Cribs.*

I walked down into the sunken living room area, where Mr. Jamison stood behind the bar fixing us a drink.

"Make yourself at home," he said as he handed me my drink.

I took my drink and sat down on this huge dark cherry-colored leather couch. I began sipping my drink and looked around the room at all the gorgeous pieces of furniture and art-work that hung on the walls. The room was definitely decorated in a manly fashion because, as nice as everything was, it was only in earth tones. No bright pastel colors needed. This was a man's home, or shall I say castle, but now that I was there, it definitely needed a diva's touch.

I noticed a fireplace on the left hand side of the wall that seemed to light on its own as Mr. Jamison flipped a switch, and a round cherry wood coffee table sat right in front of the couch. And an identical brown leather couch sat right across from the one I was sitting on.

The ceiling was so high, and it hung a huge chandelier overhead, for a minute I felt like I was in church. On the right hand side of the room, all to itself, sat an all-white upright piano with a silver candelabra on top. The paintings on the walls were not your average paintings that most black folks adorned their walls with. He had paintings of landscapes and some shit I couldn't figure out, what they called abstract art. But they all had gold-structured frames that appeared to have cost an arm and a leg.

"Ah, Cameron," Mr. Jamison uttered, interrupting my thoughts.

"Oh my bad. Did you ask me something?"

"I asked if you wanted me to take you on a tour of my home before you freshen up."

"I would love a tour." I swallowed the last of my drink and felt a little light-headed as I tried to stand.

"Maybe that drink was a little too strong for you, huh." Mr. Jamison smiled, as he grabbed me by my waist to catch me from falling.

"Naw, I'm fine."

Mr. Jamison began leading me by the hand up the spiral staircase, going from one room to another.

"How many bedrooms you have?"

"There are five bedrooms and four and a half bathrooms."

"Which bedroom will I sleep in?" I asked, hoping he would say his.

"Take your pick."

The bedrooms were so huge; one could actually live in that one room. And each one had a large flat-screen TV attached to the wall. The bedroom furniture was different for each room.

One of the bedrooms was definitely decorated with a female in mind. The white flower comforter matched the tables and dresser along with the curtains that hung from the windows and a matching ceiling fan. This was definitely the bedroom for me.

Another bedroom had masculine dark-striped wallpaper, with a dark maroon bedspread, along with matching drapes and cherry-wood furniture. The next two bedrooms had a juvenile feel to them. I didn't know if Mr. Jamison had any children or younger siblings who lived with him, but I definitely needed to find out.

The last bedroom was the master bedroom, Mr. Jamison's bedroom. I was so blown away when I entered his bedroom. Chile, had you ever seen one of the rooms where you could be happy to die in? That's the thought I had when I entered his room.

Everything in the room was white or silver. The king-size bed had a white down comforter with the initials KJ embroidered in silver right in the center, and it looked like he had fifty or so white pillows piled up at the headboard. A large movie-like screen projector TV tuned to Sports Channel hung on the wall.

*Mr. Jamison must really be into sports,* I thought to myself, considering it was on and nobody was watching it. Hell, where I was from, if you ain't watching it, it needed to be turned off, but I guess Mr. Jamison got it like that.

He also had a silver-and-white chandelier hanging from the ceiling. I don't know what it is, but it's something about chandeliers that makes a room look so elegant. Mr. Jamison also had white wooden furniture with silver trimming on the dressers, nightstands, and mirrors. Now, this wasn't like that cheap lacquer furniture, this was real wood of some kind, and I could tell he paid a good penny for it.

"Well, this is my bedroom. What do you think?" He looked at me as though he wanted to throw me on his bed and have me right then and there.

"It's fabulous."

"Not the word I would use, but I like it, too." He chuckled. "Why don't you go freshen up, and I'll make us something to eat."

"So, I can pick any room I want?"

"Yup."

"How about I choose this one?" I ran and jumped on his bed like a child.

"Sorry, shawty. You haven't earned that right yet," he replied, his arms folded in front of his chest.

"How about I earn the right now?" I started taking my clothes off.

"You got balls, shawty, I'll give you that, but that's not

what I'm talking about. So, which other room would you like?"

"I guess it would have to be the room with all the flowers," I said, disappointed.

Mr. Jamison led me back into the flowered bedroom and showed me around. The room had everything I needed, including a private bathroom area with toothbrush, soap, wash cloth, towel, and even a white thick terry cloth robe that hung on the back of the door. As he left, he closed the bathroom door behind him.

I stood looking in the mirror and thought, *This is just too good to be true.* God had finally answered my prayer in finding me a man that was beautiful.

Instead of taking a shower, I decided to take a bath since the tub was so big. I just wanted to lay my head down and relax. Everything was in here, a small flat-screen TV, a Bose AM/FM radio with CD player, and even a small refrigerator filled with soda, wine coolers, and champagne.

I ran my bathwater almost to the top of the tub and used almost all of Mr. Jamison's liquid bubble bath. Chile, I had bubbles everywhere.

I poured some champagne in one of the flute glasses that sat on top of the refrigerator and lowered myself in the tub. What was so funny was, I didn't have a dime on me, but I felt like a million bucks. I drank my champagne while listening to *The Quiet Storm* program on the radio. I was so relaxed, I drifted off to sleep.

I wasn't sure how long I had been asleep, but I knew it wasn't that long because the water was still fairly warm. Mr. Jamison awakened me. He sounded as though he was arguing with someone downstairs. I got out of the tub, dried myself off and threw on the terry cloth robe. I opened the bathroom door and tiptoed out to the main staircase leading down the steps.

I stood at the top of the stairs for a minute to see if I could make out what was being said, and all I could hear was Mr. Jamison yelling at someone about getting him his muthafuckin' money. I'd never seen him angry, nor had I ever heard him yelling at anyone, and to be honest, it kinda scared me.

I wasn't sure if I should go and stay in the room or go and see who Mr. Jamison was arguing with. My curiosity got the better of me. I tried to act as though nothing was wrong, so I walked down the spiral staircase and out into the kitchen, where Mr. Jamison stood over the stove, cooking.

He looked at me as I entered the kitchen. "Well, you look refreshed. How was your bath?"

"It was absolutely fabulous. Thank you for asking."

"You can have a seat, and I'll fix you a plate of my famous spaghetti." He pointed to a chair at his dinette set.

"Spaghetti, huh."

"Yeah. You do like spaghetti, don't you?"

"I love it. Oh, by the way, I thought I heard you talking to someone. Did they leave?"

"Oh yeah, my lil brother stopped by." He handed me my plate of spaghetti. "You just missed him."

"Were you guys arguing?"

He sat across from me with his plate of spaghetti. "Naw, not really. But sometimes I have to put him in his place, you know."

"Oh okay, I guess. So, tell me about your family."

"There's really not much to tell. Both my parents passed away a few years ago, and I promised my mom on her death bed that I would keep an eye on my younger brother. That's about it."

I was curious to know how his folks had passed. But it didn't look as though he wanted to discuss it, so I let it go for now.

"Tell me what happened. You called and asked me to come get you, but you still hadn't said what happened." He stuck his fork in his spaghetti.

I took a deep breath and began to explain what had been going on at my house with my stepfather, and the threat he'd made towards me and my sister. I also informed him that my stepfather was gay and having sex with the same guy that killed my older brother a few years earlier.

"So, this guy that killed your brother, he was never locked up?"

"Well, they caught him at the time, but he was released on bail, and then he escaped. He'd been missing for the past five years or so, and I happened to run into him at my prom. Which is fucked up, because Junior has to be at least in his mid-twenties. And he got the nerve to be hanging out at a prom."

"You said his name is Junior?"

"Yeah. Why?"

"Just wondering if you know his full name. Why hadn't you called the police to have him locked up?"

I sucked my teeth. "The police don't care about black-on-black crime. I will handle Junior myself."

"Is that right? And what are you gonna do, mister tough guy?" Mr. Jamison playfully punched me in my arm.

"Hmm, don't let this little body fool you. I don't have to use my fist." I pointed to my head. "I use this."

"You a fine shawty, and got a brain, too, huh."

"And don't you forget it," I spat, snapping my fingers and rolling my neck from side to side.

Mr. Jamison and I sat there for hours just talking and laughing. He made me feel free and allowed me to be me without questioning my manhood or lack thereof. So many gay brothers out here seemed to have such a problem with feminine gay brothas, but that didn't seem to bother Mr. Jamison at all. Because of that, I was just that much more attracted to him.

Don't misunderstand. Mr. Jamison was a fine specimen of a man anyway. He reminded me of LL Cool J, except he was a little darker, but he also licked his lips all the time just like LL and had the cutest dimples.

As I sat there and Mr. Jamison talked, I really didn't hear much of what he was saying. I wanted to jump his bones right there in the kitchen. His gentleman's fade haircut outlining his jawbone along with his trimmed mustache and goatee had me moist between my thighs.

**113**

I found myself moving around in my chair to get comfortable because my nature was rising, and not having any clothes on under this robe was making it worse.

"Are you okay?" Mr. Jamison gave me that sexy look of his.

"Ah, yeah, I'm okay." I tried to tease him by letting the left side of my robe fall off my shoulder.

He chuckled. "I see my robe seems to be a little too big for you, huh."

"Well, I can't help that my body is smaller than yours," I said, batting my eyes and crossing my legs.

He smiled and shook his head. "Come on, shawty, it's getting late. Let's go to bed."

I followed him up the spiral staircase but wasn't sure whether he was inviting me to his bedroom or not, but I was hoping and praying that he was, with each step I took.

We got to the top of the stairs, and Mr. Jamison stopped.

"Yo, shawty, I hope you sleep well." He gave me a goodnight hug and made a right down the hallway to his master bedroom.

Chile, I was so disappointed that Mr. Jamison didn't want me as much as I wanted him, I felt like crying. I lowered my head and went to the flowered bedroom, got into bed, and pulled the covers over my head.

At some point, I drifted off to sleep but had one nightmare after another. I kept dreaming about my brother Ray and how he was murdered. I was so angry and hurt, all I could do was cry out in my sleep.

"Hey, shawty, you a'ight?" Mr. Jamison asked, shaking me out of my nightmare.

Even though Mr. Jamison had awakened me, I still couldn't stop crying. For some reason, I couldn't answer his question. I just lay there crying and rocking myself back and forth.

I guess Mr. Jamison felt sorry for me and climbed in bed and held me in his arms until I fell back off to sleep. At that point, I felt so wanted, comfortable, and safe, within minutes, I was in heaven, dreaming about my new life with my new man.

*

The morning sun came shining through the window drapes, almost blinding me. When I turned to see if Mr. Jamison was still laying beside me, a smile crept upon my face as I watched him still asleep.

I quietly stepped out of bed, being careful not to disturb him, and went into the bathroom to freshen myself up. Honey, ain't nothing worse than waking up to someone with sleep in their eyes and drool running down their mouth, but chile boo, that wasn't me.

I went back into the room and stood over Mr. Jamison as he lay there sleeping with no top on and showing muscles in his biceps and a well-defined six-pack. His hairy physique was causing my young body to literally ache. I eased back the covers to get a full view and noticed his manhood as stiff as a board, peeking through his silk boxer shorts.

Chile, I know this is gonna sound like some tired-ass porn, but my mouth began to water something fierce. Maybe my eyes were playing tricks on me, but I could swear I saw his dick throbbing. As Mr. Jamison lay still on his back, I eased up from the foot of the bed and slowly took the full nine inches of his manhood out and placed it in my hot, throbbing mouth. He moaned but still lay completely still.

As I began to massage his manhood in my mouth, I looked up at him and noticed that he seemed to have a smile on his face. I took that to mean that he was aware of what I was doing and that he was enjoying it. So, I continued to deep-throat him because I wanted his hot nut to trickle down my throat.

I wanted him to fall in love with me, and I was willing to do whatever it took to make that happen. I was so turned on, I took him out of my mouth and just held his manhood in my hand. God, this man's dick was beautiful. I had never seen such a pretty dick in my entire life. His manhood was silky smooth to the touch, circumcised, thick, a beautiful mahogany color, and his pre-cum was sweet to the taste.

I had to laugh to myself as I thought about Mr. Jamison being an all-day sucker.

I placed his dick back in my mouth as I kneeled over him and swallowed him down to his balls. I felt him squirming and he began to grind his torso, trying to go deeper in my throat.

I loved having Mr. Jamison in my mouth. I had thought about this moment ever since I was a student in his class.

He continued to gyrate his torso, and I began sucking him harder because I knew he was on the verge of coming. Being so turned on, I felt my mouth water that much more.

I looked up at Mr. Jamison, and he grabbed the back of my head and rammed his manhood so far to the back of my throat, I literarily gagged.

Once I regained control of my throat muscles, I let him ram his manhood again. I felt his cum trickling down my throat and heard his moans, which sent chills down my spine. I licked every drop of his sweet nut as he continued to moan and groan and call out my name.

"Yo, shawty! Dayum, shawty!"

Well, that wasn't exactly my name, but it sounded just as good, you know.

"Why did you do that?" Keith asked, raising his voice at me.

"What do you mean?"

"What do you mean, what do I mean?" he said angrily. He got up from the bed. "Why did you suck my dick?"

"I thought that's what you wanted."

"Yo man, if that's what I wanted to do, I would have initiated it. I'm the aggressor, a'ight? So don't come at me like that, you understand?" he spat, pointing his finger in my face.

I was devastated. "Yes, sir."

Mr. Jamison left my room and slammed the door behind him. Honey, I was so hurt and embarrassed, I didn't know what to do.

**116**

I climbed back up on the bed and put the covers over my head. It seemed as though the only peace I felt was when I was asleep, as long as I didn't have any bad dreams. But, as I lay here, all I could think about was how my brother had taught me how to make a man feel good. But he'd never taught me how to make a man want me.

# Chapter 14

Several hours later, feeling depressed, I must have fallen back off to sleep because I heard the faint sound of someone knocking on the bedroom door.

"Who is it?" I asked, sitting up in the bed.

"It's me." Mr. Jamison opened the door and peeked in. "Can I come in?"

"It's your house."

Mr. Jamison entered the room and sat on the side of the bed and handed me a small silver box with a red bow wrapped around it.

I looked at the box. "What is this?"

"It's for you, a peace offering," he replied, smiling at me.

I opened the box and saw a silver herringbone chain with a small silver cross that had a diamond in the center. "It's beautiful," I responded, a big smile on my face.

"Here, let me help you put it on." He placed the chain around my neck. He then looked at me and said, "Look, Cameron, I'm sorry for what I said earlier. I meant every word of it, but I didn't mean to hurt you. So, for that, I apologize."

He then held my hand. "Yo, shawty, you're very special,

and I like you a lot. You're young though, but fine as hell. I can't help myself, but if we start this between us, we have to do it the right way."

"Yeah for the right way," I squealed, as I jumped over on Mr. Jamison, and we both fell off the bed and onto the floor.

"Whoa," Mr. Jamison responded as we both crashed on the floor. "You get excited easily, I see."

"I'm sorry, but yeah, I do. Thank you, thank you, thank you." I kissed every inch of his face.

"You're welcome, welcome, welcome." He laughed.

Then he rolled on top of me and said, "I have to run a few errands, so I'll be out for a few hours. I left a house key and a key to one of my cars along with some money down on the kitchen table, just in case you wanted to go out and buy some clothes to wear or something. We will talk later when I get back, okay."

He leaned down and kissed me so passionately, tongue and all, and it reminded me of the way he'd kissed me when we were at the club, and chile, I threw my legs around him for dear life. I never wanted to let him go. Mr. Jamison was a man, a gorgeous man, a beautiful man, and most importantly, my man.

*

Over the next few weeks I had become very comfortable living with Mr. Jamison, and I had learned quite a bit about him. I learned his habits, his schedule, what he liked, what he didn't like, and his style of clothing, which was anything from business to hood. I really liked the versatility, because he looked damn good in both.

Every morning I thought, *Would today be the day?* I guess I should explain that. You see, when Mr. Jamison said that he wanted to do things the right way, he was referring to two things. He wanted to see if I was wifey material, and for us both to be checked for any STDs, as well as HIV status. And, no, I wasn't concerned about being positive for any of that because I had only been with a few guys. And I was definitely wifey material because I cooked, cleaned, washed, and vacuumed every day to make this mansion into my home.

We hadn't had sex yet because we were still waiting on our test results. I'd never taken an HIV test before, so I didn't know how long it was supposed to take. But it had only been a few weeks. After all, I'd waited this long, so I could've waited a little while longer, right? And, besides, Mr. Jamison was the kind of man that most bitches dreamed about, so I was going to do whatever I could to keep him happy.

I used to wonder what he was doing when he didn't come home until three, four, sometimes five o'clock in the morning, but I knew he was working and I didn't wanna nag him. I'd seen so many women nag their boyfriends or husbands to the point where the man just up and left them, and then they sat there wondering why.

Bitches, leave your man alone. Even at eighteen, I knew that all your man wanted was for you to cook, clean, and fuck his brains out. Duh? And as long as you did that, it's nothing that that man won't do for you in return.

So, even though I wondered from time to time whether he was cheating, I wasn't worried because I knew as soon as our test results came back, it was gonna take Jesus Christ himself to keep me off of his fine ass. I had planned to fuck him so good, he wasn't gonna remember his own name, let alone the names of those other bitches he might've been fuckin' wit.

Mr. Jamison talked about his little brother from time to time, and they argued a lot, but I was yet to meet him. Every time I walked through the door, he always said, "You just missed him."

Now, honey, I ain't no dummy. Either, he thought I might be more interested in his brother, or he hadn't told him about our relationship. It had to be one or the other. I didn't push the issue because I know that every man who goes through this type of lifestyle faces a journey, and everyone's journey is not at the same pace. But, as they say, anyone worth having is worth waiting for.

So, chile, I had no reason to complain because, other than making a home for me and Mr. Jamison, I spent my days shopping, talking to my little sister on the phone, jamming and lip-synching to my Patti Labelle CDs, and hanging out with my girl Robin whenever she took time out from her studies.

When I told her I had actually moved in with Mr. Jamison, she almost gagged. But she had been very supportive, unlike my mom. That's why I was in the process of getting ready to go over to my mom's house so we can talk. I hadn't seen her since I'd been staying with Mr. Jamison, and she didn't understand why I moved out. Well, I was gonna tell her why today.

\*

I pulled up at my mom's house and parked out on the street. I didn't see my stepfather's car in the driveway, and even though I could have parked there, I didn't wanna be blocked in if he came home. My mom did tell me that he would be at work all day because his full-time employee had a doctor's appointment and he had to cover his shift, but I didn't wanna take any chances.

"Hey, Mom!" I yelled as I walked through the front door. "Where are you?"

"I'm in the kitchen!" she yelled back.

I entered the kitchen, and as usual, my mom was cooking all kinds of food.

"Hey, Mom. What's going on?" I gave her a hug.

"I'm cooking dinner and fixing some food for our neighbor, Ms. Brown from next door. She lost her mother yesterday. You do remember her, don't you?"she asked with a bit of sarcasm.

"Yeah, Mom, I do remember her. I haven't been gone that long. Dang!" I sampled some of her delicious food.

"Get your dirty hands out of my pans." Mom hit me on my butt. "If you're hungry, have a seat and I'll fix you a plate."

"Yes, ma'am. You know I love your cooking anyway," I stated, taking a seat at the kitchen table. "So, how did Ms.

Brown's mother die?"

"Oh, baby, she was up there in age. I guess her heart couldn't take any more," Mom stated sadly as she began fixing me a plate.

"Oh wow! Give Ms. Brown my condolences."

While waiting for my plate, I looked around the kitchen and noticed that nothing had changed. The red flowery table-cloth, the matching red pillows that cushioned the table chairs, the white-and-red salt- and pepper-shakers that sat on the kitchen table, all remained the same.

I couldn't erase the thought of seeing my stepfather and Junior here in this kitchen having sex. I wasn't sure how my mom would react to what I was going to tell her, but I wanted her to know the truth.

"Here, sweetie. Look like you hadn't been eating," Momma stated as she placed a big plate of food in front of me. "You need some meat on them bones."

"Thanks, Mom."

My mom sat across from me drinking her cups of coffee as I stuffed myself. We talked a little bit more about our neigh-bor's loss. Then she began telling me about the family, and how Keisha was spending more time down the street with a girlfriend of hers. Personally, I was happy to hear that because Keisha was now a teenager, and I didn't want her to be abused or hurt in any way. So less time spent here in this house, the better.

"Seems like when you moved out, that's when Keisha decided to spend more time down at her friend's house. What's going on, sweetie? Why did you leave?" My mom asked, her voice cracking.

"Momma, I want you to know that this is very hard for me. After Mother was placed in an institution, you're the only one that opened your home for me and Keisha, and I will always love you for that." I leaned across the table and held her hand in mine and took a deep breath. "Remember when I got out of the hospital a month or so ago?"

"Yeah, of course."

"This one day I was in the house alone, or so I thought. I was hungry, and so I came downstairs to get something to eat. Before I came down the stairs, I heard voices out here in the kitchen."

"Voices? What voices? Did someone break in here?"

"Naw, Ma, it was Dad and another guy." I lowered my head and looked down at the kitchen floor.

"And was it one of your dad's friends?"

"Well, I guess you can say that."

"Look, sweetie, whatever you have to say, why don't you just come right on out and say it?" Mom held a serious expression on her face.

Just as I was about to tell my mom what had happened, I looked up, and out of nowhere my stepdad appeared in the doorway of the kitchen.

"Okay, Mom, I have to go. I'll give you a call later," I said, jumping up from the table.

Mom grabbed me by the arm. "What in the world is wrong with you? Now, you sit your little tail back down in this chair and tell me what you were about to say."

"Yeah, Cameron, tell me and your mom what's going on with you?" My stepdad took a seat at the kitchen table and stared at me as though he wanted to hurt me.

And I remembered that look all too well. It was the same look he had when I'd caught him that night with Junior and he threatened me. Suddenly, there was a ring at the front door. It almost scared the shit out of me.

"Oh Lawd. Who could that be? Sweetie, let me get the door, and I'll be right back, okay." My mom got up and answered the door.

No sooner had she left the kitchen, my stepfather shot up from his chair and grabbed me by shirt. He penned me up against the wall, saying, "I know you hadn't forgotten what I told you. You wanna have a big mouth? Go right ahead and tell your momma and see what happens."

"I wasn't going to say anything," I replied fearfully.

"You punk-ass bitch, just make sure you don't!" he stated, anger in his eyes.

At that moment, I heard Momma closing the front door. My stepfather must have heard it too because he released his grip on me.

"Lawd, if it's not one thing, it's another," Mom stated, as she came back into the kitchen.

"Well, Mom, I gotta go. I'll call you later, okay."

"Sweetie, you were about to tell me something. Now, what is it?"

"Oh, Gerdy, let the boy go. We talked, and it's a man thing, so everything is all right." My stepdad put his arm around my neck and gave me a fake hug. "Isn't it, Cameron?"

"Yeah, everything is fine," I spat, removing his arm from around my neck and heading to the front door.

*

I jumped in the car and got the hell out of there as quickly as I could. He got some nerve, calling me a punk-ass bitch. Chile boo, he the one getting fucked on the kitchen table, not me, black bastard. You know, I wasn't a hateful person, but I was wishing for my stepfather and Junior to be dead. Now!

The feeling was so strong that on the way home, I was hoping that Mr. Jamison was there. I didn't know all of what he did for a living, other than teach, but I knew he had something to do with drugs. And everybody knows that in dealing with drugs, sometimes people get killed, so maybe Mr. Jamison could get someone to kill my stepfather and Junior for me.

I pulled up at the gate, put in the security code, and the gate opened. As I drove up the brick road to the house, there was a small black car exiting. I couldn't make out who it was because the windows were tinted so dark.

I parked the car in the garage and entered the house. I stood in the kitchen with my mouth hung open. Whoever just left here had destroyed almost everything. The kitchen table was turned upside down, and cabinets hung open with broken plates and glasses scattered on the floor.

I walked into the living room, and that was in a worse condition than the kitchen. The couch was cut up, paintings on the wall were sliced up, and someone had pulled the plasma TV off the wall and thrown it on the floor, busting the screen wide open. The pedestals with busts lay shattered on the floor, along with the piano being chopped up.

Chile, I was so scared, I didn't know whether to go upstairs and check to see if Mr. Jamison was up there hurt and needed my help, or get in the car and just leave.

I took out my cell phone and called Mr. Jamison.

He picked up on the third ring. "Hello?"

"Ah, Mr. Jamison, where are you?"

"Taking care of business, shawty. What's up?"

"Ah, I just got back from visiting my mom, and the house seems to have been broken into."

"Say what?" he yelled into the phone.

"Ah, look like someone broke into the house," I stated once again.

"Stay there. I'll be there in fifteen minutes."

# Chapter 15

"Yo, shawty, where you at?" I heard Mr. Jamison yell.

"I'm upstairs," I yelled back.

Mr. Jamison climbed the stairs, and I met him in the hall-way. The strange thing was, even though I could see the anger in his eyes as we went from room to room checking out all the damage that had been done, he'd never raised his voice. I would have had a hissy fit.

The bedrooms were in complete disarray, with shit thrown everywhere, and even the mattresses were thrown off the beds. It looked as though someone was trying to find something.

"Why would someone do this?" I asked softly, to not upset him.

"I don't know, shawty, but believe me, whoever it is gonna pay," Mr. Jamison stated confidently. "By the way, did you see anybody in the area when you came home?"

"Oh yeah. As I entered inside the gate, there was this small black car coming out. I didn't know who it was because the windows were tinted, and I couldn't see inside. I just as-sumed it was your little brother or a friend of yours."

"A small black car, huh?" he asked, looking me in my

eyes.

"Yeah."

As we headed down the steps, Mr. Jamison pulled out his cell phone. I don't know who he called, but he asked the person on the phone if he knew where Kane was. Obviously, the person on the other end didn't know because Mr. Jamison yelled and said, "Find him and call me back."

I didn't know who Kane was, nor had I ever heard him mention the name. But, whoever he was, Mr. Jamison had a few choice words for him.

"Come on, shawty, let's get out of here."

"What about your place? Shouldn't we call the police or something?"

"Naw, it's cool. I'll have some friends come by and clean everything up." He opened the front door for me.

We got into Mr. Jamison car and sped off. I didn't know where he was taking me, but I really didn't care, as long as we were together.

As we drove, he had one phone call after another. Seemed as though he was talking in riddles because I really didn't understand what he was saying other than he must have found out where this Kane person was.

He responded to the other person on the phone, "Good. I know where he is now. I'll handle it." He then hung up the phone. "You mind if we make a brief stop?"

"No," I replied, not knowing what to expect.

Next thing I know, Mr. Jamison started speeding down the highway and pulled off on Route 4, made a left on Cathedral Street, and then turned into this dark, seedy-looking alley and parked.

"Look, wait here. If I'm not back in five minutes, drive off as fast as you can." He then opened the back of his Escalade and pulled out what appeared to be a few handguns.

"What's going on?" A lump formed in my throat, making it hard for me to swallow. "Why do you have a gun?"

"Yo, shawty, chill. There is something I gotta do. Now,

like I said, if I'm not back in five minutes, drive off as fast as you can, a'ight." He walked off, a black bandanna tied around his head, wifebeater, baggy jeans, and carrying two handguns, one in each hand.

Lawd Jesus! See, I didn't expect all this O.K. Corral bullshit. I just wanted to find someone to love me and protect me, and here I was sitting in a car, and my man was about to go and kill someone. Chile, this was way too much for me.

I took a deep breath, slid over to the driver's side, and tried to get my bearings, just in case I had to pull off in a hurry. As I looked about the car, I realized this was not an automatic, it was a fucking stick shift, and I didn't know how to drive a stick. Girl, you talking about being in the wrong place at the wrong time. That was the position I was in.

But then I began to realize that this is what they called being "down for your man." I knew that Mr. Jamison was involved in drugs. I wasn't that naïve. Besides, who could live that way off a teacher's salary?

I looked at my watch and noticed that four minutes had already passed and he hadn't come back yet. The car was still running because he'd never turned it off when he got out of it. He'd just left it idling.

Suddenly, I heard gunshots ring out. I looked around to see if I could hear which direction they were coming from. I looked through the rearview mirror and saw Mr. Jamison running his ass off.

He jumped in the passenger side of the car and yelled, "Let's go, let's go!"

As nervous as I was, I placed the gear shaft in second, but as soon as I did, the car turned off.

"What the hell are you doing?" he yelled.

"I don't know."

He yelled, "Leave your dayum foot on the clutch, start this muthafucka, and let's get hell outta here!"

See, I don't know about you, but I can't understand a word of what someone is saying if they are yelling at me. Chile, my brain don't work that way.

I somehow started the car back up and put it in second gear, and the next thing I knew, the car started going in reverse. I pressed the brake pedal so hard, the car jerked and shut off once again.

Mr. Jamison yelled at me, "Dayum, shawty! Can't you drive a stick?"

"No!" I yelled back.

"Fuck! Move over." He opened the passenger side and came around to the driver's side.

As I slid back over to the passenger side, I happened to notice this guy limping and coming towards us with a gun in his hand. "Mr. Jamison, that guy has a gun!"

"Duck down! I got this."

And as soon as we drove by the guy, he jumped up on the passenger side and aimed his gun right at me. Before I could blink, Mr. Jamison whipped his gun out and shot this man dead in the face, and blood splattered everywhere, even on me.

Honey, I screamed so loud, Mr. Jamison had to stuff my mouth with a towel he had laying on the backseat of his car. To this day, I still wake up in cold sweats remembering the look on that guy's face that was half blown off.

Fortunately, we made it back on the highway unharmed. I took the towel out of my mouth and started crying like a little bitch, you hear me? Snot flew out my nose, and my tears mixed with that dead guy's blood all over my face and shirt. Baby, I was too through.

"Calm down, shawty," Mr. Jamison kept telling me while driving. "Everything is gonna be a'ight."

Things seemed to happen so fast, I couldn't get out what I was feeling or what I wanted to say. I had such a lump in my throat, and I couldn't stop shaking. Nothing I was trying to say made any sense. So, I sat there in the passenger seat, crying and shaking like I was having an epileptic fit.

Mr. Jamison pulled up to an Embassy Suites Hotel off Route 4 and parked the car in the parking lot. "Look, shawty,

I'm sorry you had to be a part of that, but I don't like being fucked with, you know. The people who broke in my house work for this nigga that goes by the name Kane. We've been enemies for a long time, but he really fucked up when he trashed my house. So, I had to do what I had to do. You do understand that, don't you?"

"I don't know," I managed to say, sounding like a child.

"Shawty, I want you to understand. I'm in this shit kinda deep, a'ight, and I need to know that you gonna have my back when shit go down. You feel me?"

I whimpered, "Y-yeah."

"Good. So check this out. We gonna crash here for a few days or so, until I get my placed cleaned up and change the security code. Is that cool?"

I nodded my head up and down. "Uh-huh."

"You're okay with this, right?" he said, staring at me. "I mean, you're sitting here shaking and crying like a little kid."

It's funny. As soon as Mr. Jamison said that, I realized just how much I cared for him and wanted to be with him. And the last thing I wanted him to think of me as a child. So if that meant I had to suck it up, then that's what I was going to do.

I instantly stopped crying and wiped my face, and my shakes went away. I pulled my tear- and blood-stained shirt off, pulled my hair back into a ponytail, and looked him dead in the eye. "Why are we still sitting in the car?"

"Well, dayum, shawty!" he said, surprised by my reaction. "It's like that now?"

"Yeah, it's like that!" I responded, moving my neck from side to side.

"Well, sit here, and I'll go get us a room, mister I-got-it-like-that-now!" He chuckled while getting out of the car. "Oh, by the way, look in the trunk and get one of my tees out and put it on."

Mr. Jamison had gone into the hotel to get us a room, and as instructed, I opened the trunk and found two identical dark blue Nike gym bags. I opened the first one and was shocked to see it was filled with a white powder individually wrapped in clear bags.

I quickly closed the bag and opened the second gym bag. It wasn't filled with drugs, but stacks of hundred-dollar bills. *Lawd have mercy!* I'd never seen so much money in all my life.

I quickly closed it as well and noticed a stack of brand-new white T-shirts folded lying over in the corner of the trunk. I grabbed the first one and closed the trunk of the car. I looked around to see if I was being watched because I felt so paranoid. I put the XXX-size T-shirt on, and it hung on me like a dress. *God! Why is it that these brothas have to wear T-shirts three or four times their size?*

Mr. Jamison came out of the hotel office. "You ready, shawty?"

"Yes, sir," I replied, walking towards the hotel entrance. "Yo, shawty, wait up. I have to get something out of the trunk first." Mr. Jamison went in the trunk of his car, and just as I thought, he pulled out the two Nike gym bags and carried them inside the hotel room with us.

"Are you hungry?" he asked while placing the gym bags under the hotel bed.

I headed for the bathroom. "A little bit."

"Cool. I'll call for room service, a'ight," he stated, raising his voice so I could hear him through the bathroom door.

"Okay. I'll be out in a minute."

I peeled my clothes off to take a quick shower, so I could wash all the grime and smell of blood off my body.

Once I was done, I looked at myself in the mirror as I dried myself off, and oddly enough, I began thinking about my mother. My real mother. I hadn't gone to see her not once in the past four years, and I began to feel a little guilty about that.

"I need to go see her," I said to myself.

I wrapped a towel around my waist and walked out into the room. Mr. Jamison was looking out the window and checking out the view while talking on his cell phone. I turned the TV on and lay across the king-size bed.

As I flipped through the channels, I noticed a couple of envelopes lying at the foot of the bed.

"What are these?" I asked Mr. Jamison as he finished his call and sat at the end of the bed.

"I got these a couple of weeks ago. These are our HIV test results." He handed me an envelope with my name on it.

The envelope was still sealed so that told me that he didn't know the results. I opened the envelope, and just as I had expected, my results indicated that I was negative. I showed Mr. Jamison mine as he showed me his, and we both were HIV-negative.

"I'm glad, shawty. Now, we can give of each other totally." He smiled as he leaned over to kiss me, but suddenly there was a knock at the door.

I was startled. "Who could that be?"

"Chill, shawty. It's probably room service." He got up and went to the door.

And sure enough, it was room service bringing us the food that he'd ordered. Truth be told, I wasn't hungry anymore, at least not for food. I was hungry for Mr. Jamison.

The room attendant had made his exit once Mr. Jamison had tipped him. I pulled the towel I had wrapped around my waist and let it fall to the floor. I approached this man I was falling in love with.

"You're a sexy little shawty, you know that, right?" He looked deep into my eyes while grabbing me by my waist.

I wrapped my arms around his neck. "So, what about this giving of each other totally you were talking about?"

"What about the food? You're not hungry?" He placed soft kisses on my lips and neck.

I said in a whisper, while pulling off his wifebeater, "Not for food."

"Hmmm, I see. Why don't you chill for a minute while I'll take a quick shower, and then we can see just how hungry you can get?" He slapped me on the ass before making his way towards the bathroom.

Chile, I was so excited that this moment was finally about to happen, I couldn't keep still. I pranced my naked little body from one side of the room to the other. I even tried looking out of the window and checking out the view, but I couldn't see a thing, other than Mr. Jamison and his chocolate, hairy, toned body lying on top of my small, smooth yella frame. I knew this wasn't going to be just a fuck, but for the first time in my life, a man that I was in love with was going to make love to my mind and my body.

Just to set the mood, I turned the TV off and turned the radio on to one of the slow jam stations. I turned off all the lights and closed the window drapes. The room was pitch black, and I lay across the bed listening to Stephanie Mills' old jam, "Feel The Fire." echoing from the radio.

For the first time in my life, I was wishing I was a female, mainly because I wanted to be everything Mr. Jamison wanted me to be sexually. To be honest, I really didn't know how he felt about females, or whether he was one of those DL brothas, but I knew most brothas who are into drugs are also into bitches. And for the sake of being able to show more public affection, I was wishing I was a female.

"Where you at, shawty?" I heard him ask.

"I'm here, waiting on you."

"Is that right?" Mr. Jamison turned the bathroom light back on and cracked the door, to have a glimmer of light shine in the room. "There you are," he stated as he got into bed and climbed butt naked on top of me.

As he began to grind his body against mine, his natural body scent penetrated my nostrils and drove me crazy. I grabbed a hold of his muscled ass cheeks and pressed his body down on mine as hard as I could. The feel of his manly body on top of mine was worth all the pain and drama I had been through. Including the fact that he had just killed someone.

He rose up off of me and began kissing, licking, and sucking me from head to toe. Chile, my hormones were working overtime. Mr. Jamison was so gentle, tender, and passionate

**134**

with every touch to my body, I yearned to have him inside me.

To my surprise, he went down on me and started giving me head. As much as I tried to enjoy it, I couldn't. As a "total bottom," that's not what I wanted to feel.

I gathered he realized that because he gently turned me over on my stomach. He started licking the back of my ankles and worked his way up to the crack of my small bubble-butt booty, which he entered with his long, hot, moist tongue, and the sensation sent chills all over my body.

I wanted to return the flavor, so I tried turning around, to go down on him.

"Naw, I'm not finished yet," he whispered, turning me gently back on to my stomach.

My booty was so wet, it felt like there was an ocean between my legs.

Mr. Jamison then lay on top of me and whispered, "Okay, shawty, turn over."

I turned over on my back and waited for further instructions.

He rose up off the bed. I couldn't see what he was doing, but he came back and whispered, "Lay back and relax your muscles. This is gonna make you feel even better."

So, I did as I was told. Because of the small glimmer of light coming from the bathroom, I noticed Mr. Jamison taking some of the white substance I saw earlier in his gym bag. He began rubbing some of it on his gums, and then he began to slowly rub some of it on the head of my penis. I wasn't sure why he wanted to do that, but within seconds, that question was answered because my breathing became heavier as my penis started to become harder and harder. Mr. Jamison then leaned down, opened his mouth and swallowed me whole.

"Lawd, Lawd, Lawd, this man here!" was all I could say. I had never had anyone give me head before, and quite frankly, I'd really never cared to have it done. But Mr. Jamison was making my body crave and yearn for anything and everything. His mouth slid up and down on my little dick as though he was sucking on an oversize clitoris, or at least in my mind, that's what I envisioned.

He then arched my back by propping some pillows behind me. He placed two of his fingers in the clear bag for some more of the white substance and began fingering my hole with it. At one point, my breathing had become so erratic and my heart was beating so fast, I thought it was gonna bounce clear out of my chest.

Suddenly, the pounding in my chest calmed down, and my booty hole began to throb, pulsate, itch, opening, closing, yearning, craving. I had never in my life felt the need or desire to have a dick up in me as much as I did at this very moment. This man was causing me to want him more than life itself.

"Please, please, give it to me," I whispered, holding on to his throbbing manhood in my right hand.

"You sure you ready," he whispered back.

"Yes, yes, yes."

He then got up from the bed and literarily picked me up in one swift motion as though I was a rag doll, pinned my back up against the wall, and slowly began inserting himself into my throbbing hole.

I truly wish I could seriously express the feeling that surged through my body as Mr. Jamison slowly and gently ground his manhood in and out of me. It was raw and aggressive, yet tender. He passionately planted soft kisses on my lips as well as whispered sweet nothings in my ear. His hot breath along my neck sent chills through my body. His dick was the perfect size, reaching places inside me I never knew I would yearn for, even to this day.

Mr. Jamison and I made love to each other and tried every possible position there was until the break of dawn. And even though I don't remember how many times he climaxed, because I lost count after the fifth time, I will always remember that he was the first man to bring me to my first climax. I fell in love that night, and so did he, or so he pretended.

For the next few days, Keith and I stayed at the hotel

waiting for this sanitation company he knew to finish cleaning up his house. I didn't mind because it gave us some real time alone. Don't get me wrong, he still handled his business and would go out in the evening, but he always came back before midnight.

I would stay up and wait for him with little surprises. For example, the second night we were there, when he came in, I had rose petals scattered from the front door into the bathroom and leading into the tub. I bathed him all over, I had room service send up a four-course meal, and after we ate, I massaged his body from head to toe. Then we made love for the rest of the night.

The third night when he entered the room, I literally raped him. I didn't give him a chance to say or do anything. I took all his clothes off and threw him down on one of the chairs in the living room area. And with my sweat socks, I tied his left hand to the left side of the chair, and then I tied the right hand to the right hand side of the chair.

At first he looked at me like I was crazy, but I told him, "Relax. This is gonna make you feel even better."

I think he knew what I was up to at that point because he smiled as I pulled out some of the cocaine he had left from the other night and began to place some of it on the head of his penis. And we made love for the rest of the night.

# $\mathscr{C}$hapter 16

Over the next few weeks back at the mansion, I seldom got a chance to see Keith. He was always out taking care of business or out fucking some bitch. I say that because in the process of getting the mansion back in order, I cleaned, vacuumed, washed everything in sight, and in doing so, I came across some criminating evidence. Evidence that proved he was fucking around on me.

I found phone numbers on book matches as well as nude pictures he had of some of his bitches, black and white alike, hidden in the back of his closet. He also had the nerve to have another cell phone, which I never knew anything about, until I happened to get the bill in the mail a few days ago. I never told him about the bill. I just threw it away and programmed the number in my phone, just in case I ever needed it. The sad thing is, I was still in love with him.

I didn't feel like moping around the house all day, so I called my baby sister Keisha to see if she wanted to hang out. Much to my surprise, she did.

*

I picked Keisha up at her friend girl's house because I

didn't wanna pick her up from Mom's house just in case my stepfather was there. We still weren't speaking. And even though my relationship with Keith wasn't as strong as I wanted to be, I still entertained the thought of him killing my stepfather and Junior for me.

Actually, when I'd first mentioned to Keith the problems I was having with my stepdad and Junior, he stated, "Just tell me when and where."

As angry as I was at what they both had done to me, I still hadn't given him a place and a time. But I was still considering it.

"Hey, big brother," Keisha stated, knocking on the passenger side window and interrupting my thoughts.

I unlocked the passenger side door. "Well, don't you look all grown up."

"Look? I *am* grown up, humph."

"You're only thirteen, girl. You ain't grown." I checked out her hoochie outfit and her face that someone tried to make up.

"I'll be fourteen in five days," she spat.

Little did she know, I'd remembered her birthday, and since school was gonna start up soon, I had planned to take her shopping for some cute little outfits and school supplies. Wow, Keisha was starting senior high this year. I was so proud of her. And even though she looked like some kinda hoochie, she was growing up to be a very pretty young lady. But, Lawd knows, I really needed to give her some makeup tips, because this "burnt gobling thing" she had going on with her face wasn't working.

Keisha was talking a mile a minute, from the time she got in the car. Up until now, I really wasn't listening to all of what she was saying because, for some reason, there was a lot of traffic in both directions. I made a right, turned onto Reed Street, thinking I could avoid most of the traffic. And, just as I thought, there wasn't much traffic at all. Within minutes, I was pulling into the parking lot of the mall.

Keisha released her seat belt. "What are we doing here?"

"I thought I would take you shopping, but if you don't feel like it, we can go somewhere else." I started the car back up, teasing her.

She squealed. "Nah-huh, we going shopping, we going shopping!"

She was so much like me, all I could do was laugh. As we entered the mall, my cell phone rang. I reached into my man bag and saw it was Keith calling.

"Hi, baby."

"Yo, shawty, where you at?"

"I'm at the mall with my little sister. Why? What's up?"

"Just checking to see how you were doing and where you were. How long you're gonna be?"

"I was going to spend the day out with Keisha, but if you need me to come home, I can."

"Naw, it's cool. I know you don't get a chance to spend much time with her, so enjoy your time. Tell her I said hello."

"Okay, will do. You need me to pick up anything for you while I'm out?" I asked, being considerate.

"Naw, I'm good. Besides, I won't be home until late. Have fun, shawty."

I thought it was strange for Keith to call and not really want anything other than keep tabs on me. I smiled thinking that maybe he was beginning to care more about what I was doing and where I was. I definitely had to pick something up for him, just to let him know that I appreciated his concern.

"Come on, Cameron," Keisha said, pulling me by my arm. "Let's check out Macy's and see what sales they got."

For the next couple of hours, Keisha dragged me in one store after the other, looking and trying on almost everything she thought was fly. She practically begged me to get a few items of clothing for her, but I refused. In my opinion, she was just a little too young to be wearing some of that hoochie crap. I did buy her one outfit that was kinda hoochie, but that's only because it was really cute. I also bought her a whole makeup kit with eyeliner, brushes, foundation, and lip-gloss. You name it, it was in there. That by itself was almost a hundred dollars. But I wasn't complaining because she was my baby sister and I loved her and wanted nothing but the best for her.

We took a break and ate lunch at the food court. Keisha wanted pizza, and I got some stir fry chicken. This gave me an opportunity to talk to her and see where her head was, how things were going at home.

"How are things at home?"

"Okay, I guess. I spend most of my time over Debbie's house," she replied rocking from side to side while eating her pizza.

"Debbie's mom doesn't mind you being there so much?"

"Nope, because she says she likes having me around because I've been a good influence for her daughter." She chuckled.

"Good influence, how?"

"I guess it's because I don't mind helping around the house with the cleaning and stuff."

"Well, good for you.  So, how is Mom doing?"

"She's okay, I guess."

"You guess?" I said sternly. "When was the last time you talked with her?"

"Me? When was the last time *you* talked with her?" she asked, rolling her neck from side to side.

"Touché," was all I could say. I had to be careful with little Ms. Thang, who was more like me than I thought.

Just as I was about to ask her about our real mother, her cell phone rang. I sat and listened to her talk to her friend girl Debbie, going on and on about some boy named Little Moe, the both of them screaming and hollering like schoolgirls. I then laughed to myself. *They* are *schoolgirls.*

Once she got off the phone, she looked at me kinda strangely.

"What's wrong, Keisha?"

"I know we were gonna spend the day together, but do you mind if we cut things short?"

"Naw. What's going on?"

"Well, Debbie just told me that this guy who like me was gonna be at this birthday party and she wanted me to go along with her."

"So, you're going to crash some party for this boy?" I asked, raising my eyebrow.

"I ain't crashing the party. Debbie was invited, and she asked me to come along as her date. So, what's the matter with that?"

"Girl, there's nothing wrong with that. I'm just teasing you. Come on, get your stuff, and I'll drop you back off at Debbie's house."

"Thanks, Cameron," she stated, grabbing all of her bags. "I promise to make it up to you."

"Yeah, yeah, yeah." I chuckled. "Let's go."

*

I dropped Keisha back off at Debbie's house. I didn't have anything else to do, so I thought I would surprise my girl Robin and stop by her house. Unfortunately, once I got there, Auntie told me she wasn't home and wasn't sure where she went or when she would be back.

I wanted to stop at my mom's house just to check on her, but I didn't wanna run into my stepfather, so I headed home. Prior to going in, I stopped at the gas station to get some gas. When I got out of the car, I noticed this dude pumping gas in his vehicle. He kept staring at me. He wasn't a bad-looking dude, but he just wasn't my type.

I got out the car, slid my credit card into the pump machine, and began pumping my gas.

The guy said, "Hey, shawty. What's your name?"

"Kyle." I continued pumping my gas.

"I'm Zack," he replied arrogantly. "But you can call me Z."

"Yeah, whatever," I said under my breath.

He placed the gas pump back into its slot. "Wow, man!

**143**

Why you so mean?"

I guess I should have been flattered because this guy was coming on to me, but I wasn't. At this point in my life, I had gotten used to guys coming on to me. Years ago, I would have been flattered and interested in anyone who came on to me that I thought was cute, but not anymore. Especially, now that I was in a relationship, right?

"So, you can't even speak to a brotha, huh," he said, climbing into his SUV.

I placed the gas pump back into its slot. "I'm sorry. My mind is somewhere else."

"So, where are you heading to?"

"Home."

Zack smiled. "Can I come with you?"

"I don't think my boyfriend would like that," I spat.

"Oh dayum! My bad. Well, I tell you what, if you ever wanna hang out, give me a call." He got out of his car and handed me his card.

*Chile boo,* I thought to myself as I accepted his business card and drove off. I looked at his card, Zachary Davis, attorney-at-law.

I would have never thought he had a high school diploma, let alone a degree in law. And on top of that, he didn't look that much older than me, so I was truly impressed. I placed Zack's card in my man bag as I entered the security code and watched the iron gate open to my home.

As I pulled up to the house, Keith's car was parked in the driveway. I didn't think anything of it, even though he'd said he wouldn't be home until late. But I thought maybe he decided to come home early and get some sleep before heading out into the night.

I threw my keys up on the kitchen counter and made my way up the stairs to Keith's bedroom. I didn't wanna call out his name, not wanting to wake him up. I stood on the outside of his bedroom with my ear against the door for a minute or so and was shocked to hear the sounds of people moaning and groan-

**144**

ing.

I knew it was Keith because he always made the same sounds during sex, but I couldn't determine who the other person was, other than I knew it was some bitch. Her high-pitched moans were making me nauseous as I leaned against the door.

A teardrop ran down my cheek. I knew Keith fucked around with bitches because of the evidence I'd found, but I'd never thought he would bring that shit home.

As I slid down to the floor, I began blaming myself for not doing something right. I mean, the only reason why men mess around is because of something the other person is not doing, right? I didn't know whether to bust the door wide open and start bitching or just leave and pretend I was never here. At least if I did the latter, I could then work on myself so I could be more of whatever Keith wanted me to be.

*If I bust through the door and start screaming and yelling, Keith will never forgive me.*

Then I thought if I handled this situation maturely and opened the door, walked in, and pretended it was no big deal and possibly joined in, Keith might love me more. Besides, all men have a thing for threesomes, right? Also, the bitch inside me was dying to find out who the bitch was in there with my man.

I picked myself up from the floor and wiped my face with my hands. I took a deep breath, turned the doorknob, and walked into Keith's bedroom. I don't know who was shocked more, me or them. I caught Keith butt naked on the upswing as he was coming down and pounding the shit out of my girl, Ms. Robin Parker. I was so stunned and surprised that Robin would do that to me, my body went totally limp, and I fainted right there.

*

When I came to, I was lying in my bed, and Keith was sitting in a chair next to my bed, talking on his cell phone.

"Hey, let me call you back," he stated to whoever he was on the phone with. "So, how are you feeling?" he asked me in a genuine tone.

"How am I feeling? Keith, how could you do that to me?" I asked as tears began to form in my eyes.

"Look, shawty, I'm sorry. I just can't be totally in a homosexual relationship. I love women too."

"Keith, you really never told me about your relationships with women, but even if you do enjoy being with them, why my girl Robin?" I was trying to hold back the tears.

"Why not Robin?" he asked, a confused expression on his face.

"Because she's my friend," I replied, raising my voice. I wiped my tears away. "Or at least she was."

"Yo, shawty, we can all make this work. I care a lot for you, and I also care for Robin. Why can't we all live here and be one happy family?"

He tried to hold my hand, but I snatched it away from him.

"Are you serious?"

"Yeah. Why not?"

"Keith, I can't believe you would do something like that and then have the audacity to ask me if we all could live together like one big happy family. Naw, I can't do that." I got out of the bed and started putting my clothes on.

He approached me. "Cameron, where are you going?"

"I don't know, Keith. I just have to get out of here and be alone so I can think."

I slid into some sandals and grabbed my man bag and headed down the stairs. Keith followed right behind me. I picked up my keys from the kitchen counter.

"You can leave if you want, but you're not taking my car."

I was so numb to everything that had just happened, I threw the keys back on the kitchen counter and walked out the front door.

Fortunately, it was towards the end of August, so the weather was still rather pleasant. It wasn't until I got beyond the iron gate that I realized I didn't have anywhere to go or anyone I could even call on to come and get me. I had walked up to the main highway, and there was a gas station/convenient store on one corner and a Waffle House on the other.

I walked inside the Waffle House and noticed the time on their wall clock. A little after midnight. I took a seat in one of the booths and began looking through the menu. I hadn't eaten since earlier today when Keisha and I were at the mall. So, I thought I would order something just to stall for time.

The spunky waitress said, "Good morning. Can I get you something to drink while you look over our menu?"

"Yes.Can I have an iced tea and a number four?" I placed the menu back in its slot.

"And how would you like your eggs?"

"Scrambled, please."

"Would you like cheese in your eggs?"

"No, thank you."

"Okay, that's an iced tea with a number four. I'll bring your iced tea back in a minute, okay."

"Thank you."

I sat and looked around the restaurant, and beside me, there was only one other customer there. At first I thought he might be a psycho, the way he kept looking at me funny, but then I noticed he had a collar on and that he was a priest. He nodded in my direction, and to be nice, I nodded back.

The waitress came with my food, and I ate every bite. Chile, I didn't realize how hungry I was. The waitress asked if I wanted anything else, and I told her I didn't, so she gave me the bill and continued cleaning off some of the empty tables.

I reached in my man bag to pull out my wallet and was furious to find out that my credit card, or shall I say, Keith's credit card, wasn't there. It had dawned on me that since Keith didn't want me to drive his car, he obviously had gone in my wallet and took out everything that belonged to him, including his credit card and his money.

I looked around to see where the waitress had gone, and

for a split second, I thought maybe I should just run out without worrying about paying the nine dollars. However, something stopped me, and all of a sudden, the floodgates opened, and I began to cry hysterically, wailing and sobbing uncontrollably.

"Are you okay?" the waitress asked me.

I boo wooed, "No, no, no, no, no."

"Are you ill? Can I call someone for you?"

"I-I-I-I ain't-ain't got no-no-no one."

The priest took a seat across from me. "Young man, look at me."

I looked up at this white priest, wondering what he could possibly do to help me and wipe me of my sins.

"Young man, what is your name?" he asked.

"Cam-Cam-Cameron."

"Do you have a place to stay? Are you homeless?"

"I don't have anybody, and I don't have any money!!!!" I snapped as the tears continued to flow.

"I'm gonna call the police."

"No, it's okay. I'll pay for his meal. Look, Cameron, my name is Father Burk, and I know of a man who runs a shelter for homeless men. It's called Yes We Can, Incorporated. You can come with me, and I can take you down there to see him. He will be able to provide shelter for you, so you won't have to be out here on the streets. And you won't have to worry about the police taking you in."

Father Burk paid for my meal and escorted me out to his car. I was feeling so weak, he literally had to hold me up. One would have thought I hadn't eaten in days. I cried the whole time Father Burk drove me to my new home. I realized my weakness was from having my spirit broken and that God was paying me back for all the wrong I had done.

I slumped down in Father Burk's car thinking, *Forty-eight hours ago I lived in a mansion, drove a nice car, wore all the latest fashions, and had money in my pockets. Now I'm homeless and alone.*

# Chapter 17

Yes We Can, Inc. occupied a run-down two-story brick building located in what they considered the hood area of town. If you were given permission to leave the grounds, you could leave out as early as seven a.m. and had to be back and checked in no later than ten p.m. The sleeping area was that of an open bay, with thirty-five iron-clad cots strategically placed in this one huge room. There was a bathroom on the first floor and one on the second floor. The bathrooms didn't have tubs or even a shower. There was one toilet and one sink in each of the bathrooms. Needless to say, the lines were long at times. The walls were covered in graffiti, the paint was peeling, and water stains lined the corner of the walls. They also had a kitchen area in the rear of the first floor.

Most of the food they stored was donated by community churches. Two meals were served each day, breakfast and dinner, and if you missed either one, you were shit out of luck.

There was a small office located on the right as soon as you entered the building, Mr. Webber's office. Mr. Webber was a big black guy, almost weighing 250 pounds, with a scruffy beard. He appeared to be in his early to mid-forties and seemed to get along with everyone. He always had a smile on his face, which made me wonder why.

The second day I spent at Yes We Can, Inc. was rough for me because, being one of the occupants, I had to participate in all activities, including their workshops. I attended my first NA meeting, and even though I wasn't a drug addict, I was forced to attend. We all sat in a semicircle. I was terrified hearing the stories of these men and what they had been through as a result of their addiction. Most had been married with families and nice jobs, but because of their addiction, had lost it all. Some had been on the streets for years stealing whatever they could and selling their bodies just to get that next fix.

I sat there reading over the principles of the twelve-step program which stated:

**Step One**: **We admitted we were powerless over our addiction, that our lives had become unmanageable.**

**Step Two: We came to believe that a Power greater than ourselves could restore us to sanity.**

**Step Three: We made a decision to turn our will and our lives over to the care of God as we understood Him.**

**Step Four: We made a searching and fearless moral inventory of ourselves.**

**Step Five: We admitted to God, to ourselves, and to another human being the exact nature of our wrongs.**

**Step Six: We were entirely ready to have God remove all these defects of character.**

**Step Seven: We humbly asked Him to remove our shortcomings.**

**Step Eight: We made a list of all persons we had harmed, and became willing to make amends to them all.**

**Step Nine: We made direct amends to such people wherever possible, except when to do so would injure them or others.**

**Step Ten: We continued to take personal inventory and when we were wrong promptly admitted it.**

**Step Eleven: We sought through prayer and medita-**

tion to improve our conscious contact with God as we understood Him, praying only for knowledge of His will for us and the power to carry that out.

Step Twelve: Having had a spiritual awakening as a result of these steps, we tried to carry this message to addicts, and to practice these principles in all our affairs.

Not to be funny, but I was thinking how nice it would be if there was something like a twelve-step program in being gay, primarily, a twelve-step program in the rules and bylaws of gayhood. Hmm.

Anyway I listened to the tragic yet inspiring stories of these brothas who at times would break down and cry. This one dude stood up and began telling his story. To make a long story short, he stated that he would stay high all the time on crack cocaine. He would stay in the house and was so paranoid. Every strange or unusual sound he heard, he would run into his living room and peek out his living room window to see if Santa Claus was actually coming to see him. He stated that since he didn't have a fireplace in his home, he thought Santa would come and knock on his front door, not to hurt him but bring him his next fix.

Chile, I laughed so hard, I was literally asked to leave the meeting.

I truly felt sorry for these people. They scared the shit out of me. I was the youngest one here, and it was quite obvious to everyone that I was a feminine gay man. Now, most would have tried to butch it up, but I wasn't gonna try to be something or someone I wasn't.

I mentioned to Mr. Webber that some of the men were making threats and advances toward me, but he said there wasn't anything he could do until something actually happened. He stated that brothas in here threatened each other all the time, but ninety-nine percent of the time, they were just mouthing off, doing what a lot of men did, wanting to be the alpha male in an all-male environment.

The worst time was at night because during the day, there

was always something planned for us to do. Also, there was always someone in charge who could make sure nothing happened that wasn't supposed to happen. Some of the occupants actually had daytime jobs and would leave in the morning and not come back until the evening.

I wanted to sleep somewhere closer to the walls, to avoid having anyone on either side of me, but I wasn't that fortunate. The only cot left was in the middle of the room, with a bum that stunk to high heaven on one side, and a known drug addict, thief, rapist, and bully on the other.

The first time I met him, he uttered out of his mouth, "Yo, man, you look like a bitch," grabbing his crotch and looking at me wide-eyed.

I woke up early the next morning and found myself on my stomach, though I usually slept on my side. The covers were pulled off me, and my underwear was down by my knees, and this known drug addict was standing over top of me, masturbating. I was so scared, I screamed as loud as I could, while trying to pull my underwear back up on me.

I woke up everyone in the building. They all looked at me as though I was crazy. Of course, the drug addict jumped back in his bed and acted like he didn't know what was going on.

The night monitor escorted me into Mr. Webber's office to ask me questions so that he could make out a report. I told the night monitor what had happened and answered all of his questions, but he acted as though he didn't believe one word I'd said. Once the interview was over, I went back to my cot, threw my covers around me, and rocked myself back and forth until daybreak. I knew from that point on that I would never be able to sleep in this place.

The next morning I was summoned to Mr. Webber's office. I couldn't wait to talk to him and let him know what had happened, thinking he could make arrangements somehow for me to switch cots with someone, preferably someone who slept on the second floor, since I wanted to be as far away as possible from that goon.

Mr. Webber told me that, technically, no crime had been committed. As for switching cots, that wasn't possible either.

"If I try to change someone's sleeping area, that would cause confusion."

*Confusion?* What the fuck was he talking about, confusion? He would prefer me to be harmed or raped than to cause confusion?

There was no way I could stay here another night. After leaving Mr. Webber's office, I checked myself out and walked right out the front door, not knowing where I was going.

I walked until I got tired. I stumbled upon Freedom Park and decided to sit down and rest my legs. As I sat there watching people go on with their daily lives, I began to feel sorry for myself. I had no money and no place to go. I guess you could say, I had my own pity party going on.

I kept thinking about all the things I had been through up until this point. My spirit was still broken, and my faith was gone, so I couldn't even ask God to forgive me or even help me. I had to start helping myself.

I began thinking about Keith and what he expected from me. I tried to weigh the pros and the cons. Bottom line was, I'd rather live in a mansion, have a full stomach, and have money in my pocket than to be homeless and broke. Thank goodness for the shelters and the churches that supported them, but it wasn't the place for me.

I decided to put my pride aside and figure out a way to crawl back to Keith. I pulled my cell phone out of my man bag and called his number.

He answered his phone on the second ring. "Hey, shawty. What's up?"

"Ah, can you come get me?" I said in a whisper.

"Where you at?"

"I'm over at Freedom Park, by the water fountains, on South Twenty-Fourth Street. You gonna come get me?"

"Yeah, shawty. I'll be there in twenty minutes."

I was so excited to actually be going back to the mansion and having a soft comfortable bed to lay in, a tub full of bubbles, a large flat-screen TV with over 200 channels to view, my Patti Labelle CD collection, and last but not least, a delicacy of food to nourish my body. I felt like I'd been gone for weeks, and it had only been a couple of days.

I know that most could care less about these things but for me, I had to have them. Even if I had to sell my soul to the devil, so be it. God truly didn't seem to care for me or my soul, so why not give Satan a chance? It sure beat the hell out of living in a shelter, chile boo.

Suddenly, I realized I had on the same jeans and T-shirt I had on when I'd left Keith's house. *Oh my God! What will he think?*

I pulled out my compact and I looked a hot mess. I needed my braids redone because my hair was all over my head, I could use a serious facial treatment, and a manicure wouldn't have hurt either.

I heard a horn honk and looked over my compact and saw Keith sitting in his Escalade, looking some kinda good in his "yo boy outfit" and sunglasses.

I got in the passenger side. "Thanks for coming and picking me up, Keith."

"No problem, shawty. Where you been?"

"It's a long story," I replied, sitting back and getting comfortable in the cushioned leather seats. "I just need a nice hot bath."

"Oh, okay. I have missed you."

"Really, Keith?"

He looked deep into my eyes. "Of course, I have."

I was so turned on by his comment. Not only that, it made me feel good about myself, and I know he meant every word because, if not, he wouldn't have said it.

\*

We pulled up to the gate, and Keith put his code in, and

we drove up to the entrance.

Like I said before, I felt as though I had been gone for weeks. I couldn't wait to get to my bedroom, rip these clothes off, and take a nice hot bath. Once we got inside, I was so surprised to see a big banner at the top of the stairs that literally took my breath away. It read, *Welcome Home Shawty.*

"How did you?" I asked, smiling from ear to ear.

"I had it made and hung the same day you left, shawty."

Standing in the back of me, he placed his arms around my waist. I leaned my head back on his chest, wrapped my hands around his, and I truly felt safe, secured, and loved.

Keith spent the whole day with me, cooked me a huge breakfast, ran my bathwater with lots of bubbles, bathed me from head to toe, and cuddled with me in my bed as we watched reruns of *The Golden Girls.*

*I know that's so gay, but I love them three white dragons. Chile, what can I say?*

Keith and I talked and laughed so much, we became so exhausted, we fell asleep in each other's arms.

I must have been really tired because I didn't wake up until the next morning, and Keith was still lying beside me, asleep.

*Maybe this could work? Besides, people make sacrifices in their relationship all the time, don't they?*

I truly loved Keith because no other man ever made me feel the way he did, emotionally or physically. Even now as I lay here looking at him sleep, I can't help but try to be everything he wanted me to be.

Keith made me so aroused just by looking at him sleeping. I needed and wanted him inside me.

I pulled the covers back, crawled between his legs, and took him in my hungry mouth.

For the next couple of hours, no one else existed. He and I made tender, passionate love to each other as though we were the only two people in the entire world.

I was happy and in love again.

**155**

# Chapter 18

A few days later, Keith was right back at doing his own thing. But I wasn't going to complain. I had my car back, money in my bag, and two of his Visa Black cards, so I was good to go.

I had been trying all morning to contact my little sister Keisha because today was her birthday. I wanted to take her out and celebrate, but she wouldn't answer her phone. I left a message to let her know to call me, that it was important.

*Wow! My little sister is fourteen years old, a young lady.* I smiled, thinking back about how much she used to get on my last nerve.

While waiting on Keisha to return my call, I fixed me a tuna fish sandwich along with some chips and began watching one of the morning talk shows. They had this woman on the show that had forgiven this young guy who had killed her one and only son. On top of that, she somewhat spearheaded his release from jail, even though he was convicted and sitting on death row. The murder had taken place more than twenty years earlier, but this woman actually forgave this guy and now lived right next door to him.

Of course, they'd both had time to think about what happened so many years ago, but to forgive him and accept him, not only as a neighbor, but to actually allow him to call her "Mom" was a bit much.

It did cause me to think more about my real mother and how bad I felt for not visiting her once within the past four and a half years since she'd been committed. I suddenly had the urge to see her. I wasn't sure what I would say to her, but I just wanted to see if she had aged and if there was anything I could do for her. That show had caused me to feel real sentimental. I was ready to forgive my mother for zoning out on me and Keisha.

I couldn't remember the name of the mental institution. So, I got on Keith's computer downstairs in his office, logged on, and checked Google for all mental institutions in the area. I was thinking, once I saw the name, that would help me remember. Only two popped up, but Crownsville Mental Institution rang a bell. I clicked on its Web site and wrote down the number and address.

As I closed the Web site, I noticed that Keith had several Web sites still open, but minimized down at the bottom of his computer.

I restored the first one, a porn site with big breasted and big bubble-butt mommas. "Ewww! Freak," I said to myself."

I restored the second Web site, Yahoo! Messenger. Keith was having a conversation with a person named Jermaine "Junior" Rogers. Jermaine Rogers was the same name of the bastard who killed my brother, who also went by the name Junior.

I suddenly got a sickness in my stomach and felt as though I was about to throw up. My body began shaking. Even my hands were shaking on the keyboard as I tried to scroll to the top of the page where the conversation began.

Jermaine "Junior" Rogers: Hey bruh, you get that package last night?

Keith "I Got This" Jamison: Dayum skippy

Jermaine "Junior" Rogers: Good looking out bruh

**158**

**Keith "I Got This" Jamison:** Yeah, but the next time I tell yo azz, you betta do it!

Jermaine "Junior" Rogers: Yeah bruh I will. Just got caught up in a situation. You know how it is, right? Hey btw, shawty back?

**Keith "I Got This" Jamison:** Yeah man, he called me and I went and picked his ass up a couple days ago. He's here now, knocked the fuck out. Lol

Jermaine "Junior" Rogers: Wow, again good looking out. He still don't know you're my brother, right?

**Keith "I Got This" Jamison:** Hell no, you just need to chill. I got this, a'ight?

Chile, if I had pearls around my neck, I would have clutched them. My heart sank finding out that Junior was Keith's little brother. And in spite of Keith's sexual confusion, I really believed he loved me. Now finding out that this was just a game hurt me to my core. Honey, I was so mad, I wanted to throw his computer out of the window. But, as angry as I was, I continued reading.

Jermaine "Junior" Rogers: Ok Ok Big Bruh, I'll just lay low until you give me the word, a'ight?

**Keith "I Got This" Jamison:** You do that. How's the sister?

Jermaine "Junior" Rogers: yeah I got dat little bitch nose wide open bruh. Lol

**Keith "I Got This" Jamison:** kewl, you hit it yet?

Jermaine "Junior" Rogers: Not yet, not really.

**Keith "I Got This" Jamison:** What u mean not really, yes or no muthafucka.

Jermaine "Junior" Rogers: I ain't fucked her yet but I did lick her young pussy and Bruh she went crazy. She wanted me to fuck her right in her momma house too. Lol

**Keith "I Got This" Jamison:** Why didn't you? Don't

**tell me you were scared of that young pussy?**

I'd had enough. I couldn't read another word. I minimized the screen back down to the bottom of the page and left the computer exactly the way I found it. I was so mad, I wanted to kill the both of them.

I jumped up from the table, ran back upstairs to my room, and slammed my door.

I paced the floor from one side of the room to the other, trying to get Keisha on the phone. Again, she didn't answer.

"Oooo, I swear, I'ma wring that girl's neck when I see her," I said to myself as I continued to pace the floor. You can fuck with me all you want but my sister? Oh, hell naw! I needed some help, but who could I call?

I thought about calling my mom. *If I tell her what I just found out, she would worry herself to death.* I grabbed my bag and raced down the steps, going as fast as I could.

I got into my car and went over to Debbie's house, hoping my sister would be there. I made it there in record time, and based on what Debbie's mother told me, she wasn't there. Both her and Debbie left out and didn't tell her where they were going.

*Oh please! What mother in their right frame of mind don't find out where their child is going?*

I sat in the car, trying to figure out where Keisha and her friend might have gone. They could have gone anywhere…the mall, the movies, downtown, or even to the park.

I pulled out my cell phone and tried to call her again, but it went straight to voice mail. *Fuck!*

Having nowhere else to go and not wanting to go home, I pulled the address to the mental hospital where my real mom was staying out of my bag and input the information into my GPS.

\*

It took me about forty-five minutes or so to get there, but I didn't mind because it gave me time to think about what I wanted to say to her. I started wondering whether she would remember me or whether she even looked the same and what state of mind she was actually in. I pulled into the visitors' parking lot, got out of the car, and headed to the main entrance.

The security guard stated to the visitors standing in line and waiting to go through a metal detector, "Please place everything in your pockets into the bowl, including your belts, purses, watches, coins, and anything that may be metal."

Dayum! I didn't realize you had to go through all this. Fortunately, I didn't have anything on me except for my keys because I'd left my bag in the trunk of my car. I dropped my car keys in the bowl and walked through without a hitch and proceeded to the information counter.

"Who are you here to see?"

"Ms. Janet Wilson."

"And you are?"

"I'm her son, Cameron Jenkins—I mean, Cameron Wilson."

"Do you have any ID?"

I pulled out my driver's license from my back pocket. "Here."

"Okay, Mr. Wilson, have a seat, and we will let you know when she has come down."

I took a seat in the waiting room along with several other people who, I'm sure, were waiting to see their loved ones as well. As I looked around, I was happy to see the facility appeared very clean. The checkered-board floors were spotless with a high glossy finish, and the walls were painted a bright white.

I grabbed one of the pamphlets and starting reading what they did at the facility. According to the pamphlet, the facility held over 175 patients, a full-time medical staff of 50 on duty 24 hours a day, and 14 psychologists.

"Mr. Wilson."

"Here." I got up out of my seat and walked over to the information desk.

One of the security officers told me, "Your mom is in

room four. Walk this way."

One of the attendants behind the information desk pressed a button, and the lock door on the left hand side of the information counter opened. I followed the security guard down this long corridor. We stopped in front of this padded cell, he swiped a card, and the door automatically opened.

I walked in and saw this woman slumped over in a chair, her head down. It didn't look as though her hair had been done in years, because it was all over her head, along with several matted spots.

I took a seat across from her and tried to look into her eyes, but she wouldn't raise her head. "Mother, this is Cameron. Are you okay?" I stated in a heartfelt tone.

"Don't waste your time, man," the security guy told me. "She don't talk."

"What do you mean, she doesn't talk?" I asked him.

"She hasn't uttered five words since she's been here. No one knows why."

"Can I spend some time alone with her, please?"

"No problem. You have an hour. If you want to leave before then, just press this button next to the door, all right."

"Thank you," I responded as he left the room.

I focused my attention back on my mother. I turned and faced her. "Mom, can you talk to me?" I waited for her to answer, but she said nothing as she sat there with her head hung low.

I didn't know if she could hear me, but I told her everything that had been going on for the past four years. I also told her what had been going on with Gerdy, her new husband, and the threats he made towards me and my sister, about Keshia and her grown ass, Ray's murderer, Junior, who I just found out was Keith's brother, and still roaming the streets, and my best friend Robin, who had started sleeping with my boyfriend Keith.

At times I saw her facial expression turn into a smile and then a frown as I told her what had been happening.

Once I was through, I sat there waiting for her to respond, I mean, say something, anything. But she didn't.

"Momma, say something." Tears began to flow down my cheeks. "Momma, can you even hear me? Momma, talk to me, please. I need your help. There's no one else I can turn to. And I'm sorry I hadn't come to visit you until now but, Momma, please, I need your advice on what I should do."

I sat there staring at her, waiting for a response. I lowered my head on the table and cried my eyes out. I was so hurt that even my mother wouldn't try to comfort me or even help me.

I was so tired, just tired of everything and everyone. I raised my head and wiped the tears from my eyes. "Okay, Momma, take care of yourself. And, again, I'm sorry." I got up from my seat and walked towards the door. I lowered my head and softly said, "And I'm sorry for not being more like Ray."

"Where are you going, boy?" my mother asked in a raspy, demanding tone.

I was so stunned, I froze for a quick second. I turned around, and my mother was standing on her feet with her head held high and her arms stretched out wide. I walked over to her sobbing, and she wrapped her arms around me.

Within those four years I had grown an inch or so taller than she. I laid my head on her shoulder and bawled my eyes out like a two-year-old. Chile, there's nothing like a warm hug from Momma. We stood there in that room with her arms around me that seemed like hours, but I didn't care. I couldn't let go, I didn't wanna let go.

"Baby, it's okay. It's gonna be all right," she said, rocking me in her arms.

We eventually sat back down at the table. My mother informed me that there was nothing wrong with her vocal cords. Some people she spoke to, others she didn't speak to. The latter thought she couldn't talk.

My mom and I talked about everything, including the fact that she was still mourning the loss of my brother Ray. She also told me not to worry, that she would take care of everything.

"Mom, how are you gonna take care of anything being in here?" I looked around at her padded cell.

"What? You think I have to stay here?"

"Yeah. Well, don't you?"

"My poor baby. No, Cameron, I don't. I've been here because of my own accord. I can leave whenever I want."

"So, why do you stay here, Mom?" I asked, shaking my head.

"I stay here because I have no place to go," she said softly, choking up.

I lowered my head. "I'm so sorry, Mom. I'm gonna change that, I promise."

"Don't be sorry, baby. I've doing just fine. I really have." She placed her hand on top of mine. "So, like I said, I'll take care of everything, all right."

"Well, what do you want me to do?"

Momma sat back in the chair with her arms folded. "Baby, all I need you to do is get me in the house. I'll do the rest."

"But, Momma, what are you going to do? I mean, what else can I do?"

"Baby, like I said, just get me in the house."

# Chapter 19

A couple of months had gone by since I last visited my mother. Since that time, our relationship grew like we were sisters. Yes, I said sisters. She now accepted my lifestyle, and we spent a lot of time with each other, hanging out, shopping, or whatever. The day she signed herself out of the institution, I had taken her for a makeover, got her a new wardrobe, and a new short hairdo with blonde streaks. And, chile, my momma looked some kinda good, you hear me? Still a young woman of forty-five, not only was she still beautiful but smart as well.

I was able to rent out a small efficiency apartment for her, completely furnished and only twenty minutes away from the mansion. Fortunately, the rent wasn't that much.Hell, I would spend more than that on one outfit, so Keith never questioned where the money was going because he gave me a monthly allowance. He stated that anyone he was fucking had to look good, whether we went out or not.

Chile boo, anyway, I also purchased my mom a used hooptie for only five hundred bucks. It wasn't much to look at but was in very good condition, or so the previous owner stated.

As for my sister Keisha, my real mother pulled her fast behind up quick.Granted, even though my mother had been away for four years, Keisha did exactly what my mother told her to do, and she did it without bitching. Keisha now stayed with my mom most of the time, because a teenage girl definitely needs to be with her mother, no disrespect to Ms. Gerdy, who I have nothing but love for, and still see as my mother as well.

My real mom and I both felt that now wasn't a good time to inform Ms. Gerdy that my real mom was out of the institution. And Ms. Gerdy still thought that Keisha was spending her time over Debbie's house. I was truly hoping that once this was all over we would all be one big happy family, without my stepfather, of course. My real mother informed me that she knew Ms. Gerdy's husband very well and for me not to worry because she was going to get rid of him as well. I don't know what my mother had over my stepfather, but whatever it was, she kept telling me that the shit was gonna hit the fan.

Oh, and Keith finally had Ms. Fag-hag move into the mansion a couple of weeks ago. Ain't that a bitch? Anyways, she'd been walking around here like Ms. Queen Bee and shit, but I paid her no mind. At least, I tried not to.

When she'd first moved in, she didn't have much to say to me. I guess Keith noticed and spoke with her about it, because for the past few days, she'd been grinning all up in my face. Chile boo, I really ain't got shit to say to her.

And the other day, she had the audacity to come knocking on my bedroom door to see if I would help her do her makeup because she and Keith were going out. But of course by now, you know what I told her, chile boo. I will admit, it still hurt to see the one you thought you love be with someone else, but thank God for my mom, because she helped me get through this whole situation. She'd often told me that, at times, if you truly love someone, you have to learn how to let them go, blah, blah, blah.

As for Mr. Keith Jamison, I thought I loved him, but now I wasn't even sure. The only reason why I was here dealing with this situation and all the bullshit was because my mother and I planned on getting paid big time. You see, a few weeks ago, and at my mother's request, I went snooping around in Mr. Keith Jamison's office and discovered that he had a safe hidden behind one of his fake Rembrandts hanging on the wall.

And I figured out the combination. Dummy uses his birthdate for everything. "Why are guys so stupid?" I asked my momma.

She said, "Baby, they just is."

I opened the safe, and Keith had so much money and drugs in it, I almost gagged. I didn't take the time to count it because I really wasn't sure how long he would be gone. I closed the safe and ran upstairs to my bedroom to give my mother a call.

"Hey, baby. How you doing?"

"Mom, Keith has a safe in his office," I said, sounding out of breath.

Mother laughed. "Of course, he does. He sell drugs, don't he? I told you he would."

"I know, Mom, but it was so much money in there."

"Oh really? Do tell."

"Well, I don't know exactly how much was there. I didn't get a chance to count it because I didn't know how long he would be gone."

"Okay, but we also need to find out when he makes his drops. I know he must keep account of what's going out and what's coming in, so you need to find this out as well."

"Momma, but I don't know what to look for."

"All right, but have you thought of a way to get me in the house?"

"I'm still thinking how I can do that without him becoming suspicious."

"Look, baby, I tell you what. That's a big house. Tell him you would like to hire a maid. He seems to be a brotha who likes living large, and everybody knows that people with money don't clean their own shit. And I know you're tired of trying to keep that big-ass place clean by yourself, right?"

"Chile, you just don't know."

"See, so tell him you wanna hire a maid, baby."

"But who we gonna get as a maid, Mom?"

"Cameron, I'm going to be the maid," she responded, raising her voice.

"Momma, Keith may not know who you are, but Robin lives here now, and she would definitely know who you are."

"Hmmm, that's right." She hesitated before saying, "Well, since my makeover, she may not. Besides, she hasn't seen me in four years, and even you said I don't look the same."

"This is true. But I don't know, Mom. It could be very risky."

"Well, I could dress up in disguise."

"Disguise? What kinda disguise?"

"I don't know, Cameron. People disguise themselves all the time," she thought for a moment and said, "You know that movie with Martin Lawrence, *Big Momma's House*? Maybe I can disguise myself up to be Big Momma."

"Momma, you can't be serious?" I laughed hysterically.

"And why not?" she responded, laughing. "I don't do fat suits. I will do the old maid's dress and a wig, but I won't do a fat suit."

"Okay, Momma, I hear you, no fat suits," I responded, still laughing.

"What about the muthafucka that killed your brother? Does he still come around there?"

"You're talking about Junior? Yeah, he comes around, but Keith makes sure I'm never here when he comes around because he still doesn't want me know they're brothers."

"Well, Cameron, why are they playing these games?"

"Momma, all I know is that Keith told Junior that he keeps his friends close but keeps his enemies closer. I suspect that I'm the enemy because they are afraid I will have Junior arrested. And if I do that, the police will also discover their involvement with drugs and killing people," I started choking up.

"All right, Cameron, it's okay. They will get theirs. Trust Momma, you hear me?"

"Yes, ma'am."

"Now, is Keith there?"

"No."

"Is Robin there?"

"No."

"All right, baby. What I need you to do is put on some work clothes and let him see just how hard you work in keeping his shit clean. I don't care what time he gets in, he needs to see you working your fingers to the bone, and then and only then can you talk to him about hiring a maid. Once he agrees, I'll take it from there."

"Okay, Momma, I will. Tell Keisha I said hello and give her a kiss for me."

"Will do, baby. Call me tomorrow and let me know what he said."

"Okay, Momma. Love you."

"Love you too."

After we hung up, I couldn't help but smile because I was finding out that my momma was a piece of work and not to be fucked with. She was such a strong woman. I wished I could be more like her.

I opened my closet door to try to find some dirty clothes I could put on, so I could show Keith just how hard I worked in keeping his house clean. I found the old dirty jeans I had worn when I ran off to the shelter. I thought I had thrown them away because I had vowed to never wear them again. But I was glad I didn't because I couldn't find anything else. Anyway, I put them on with an old sweat shirt that I tore up.

It was a little after midnight, and I still didn't know what time Keith would be coming in. I rushed downstairs to scrub the kitchen floor and, much to my surprise, ran into Ms. Fag-hag studying at the kitchen table.

"Hi, Cameron," she stated, all perky and shit.

"Hey," I responded, not wanting to be bothered.

She looked at clock on the wall. "Why are you up so late?"

"Because these floors are filthy. And since I'm the only one around here that does any cleaning, they won't get done until I do them." I took a bucket out from the base of the kitchen sink.

"Well, Cameron, I don't see where the floors are all that dirty," she replied, looking down at the kitchen floor.

"Look, all you do around here is eat, sleep, and fuck, so mind your business, okay," I stated, rolling my neck, my hands on my hips.

"Well, I was just saying…I don't know why we can't get along. We used to be the best of friends."

"Yeah, we were. Until you started fucking my man.

She sucked her teeth. "Well, he couldn't have been much of your man if he wanted me."

I wanted to take this bucket of water with suds as I stood there at the kitchen sink and dump it over her head. But I was curious to find out why she was doing what she was doing and who made the first move.

"Why, Robin? Why would you do that to a friend like me?"

"It wasn't my intentions, Cam. It just happened." She stood up and came over to me.

"Oh, so his dick just happened to fall in your pussy by accident. Is that what you're saying?"

"No."

"So, how did it happen?"

She didn't respond, but it seemed as though she was thinking.

"I'm listening."

"Okay, you wanna know? I'll tell you. Remember that day you called me and told me you had moved in with Keith?"

"Yeah. Go on."

"Well, I had been so busy with school and with dating this guy, you and I hadn't had much time together. And my mom had told me that you had stopped by to see me a few times, but I was never there. So, this one day, I really needed to talk to you because the guy I was dating had been killed. I was so upset that I came by here to see if you were here, but you weren't. Keith answered the door and remembered who I was. He invited me in to wait for you. He saw how upset I was. I started talking to him about it, and he began comforting me. And one thing led to another."

"Oh, so now I'm supposed to feel sorry for you?" I asked, looking at her crocodile tears.

"No, but I thought you would be a little more understanding."

"Understanding? Girlfriend, if you want me to be a little bit more understanding, you need to move out, leave my man alone, and carry yo' fat ass back home."

"But I love him, and he loves me!" she screamed, as the tears continued to pour down her face.

"Chile boo, you don't know what love is," I said, getting in her face.

"Whoa!" Keith walked into the kitchen. He looked at Robin then at me. "What the hell's going on?"

"Nothing." I began to move the kitchen table to the side, so I could start scrubbing the floor.

"Robin, what's going on, babe?" he asked, wiping away her fake tears.

"Nothing, babe." She hugged him. "I'm just feeling a little emotional right now, that's all. How was your night?"

"It was good, it was good," he answered, hugging her back.

"Keith, when you get a chance, I really need to talk to you about something." I started slinging a wet mop across the floor, splashing them both.

He quickly moved out of my way. "Sure. Wassup, shawty?"

"We can talk later," I said, rolling my eyes at Robin.

"Well, whatever you gotta say to me, you can say in front

of Robin. We are one big happy family, aren't we?" He took a drink out of the refrigerator.

"Hmmm, so we are," I said, wanting to throw up. "Look, this is a big house, and I have been trying my best to keep it clean. Nobody around here helps me do that. I do most of the cooking as well as the cleaning and I'm tired."

Keith chuckled. "So, what do you want me to do, shawty? Help?"

"No, I wanna hire a maid." I wiped the sweat from my forehead.

"A maid?"

"Yes, a maid. Someone who comes in a few times a week. They cook, they clean, you pay them, and they go home. I can't keep doing this by myself."

"Yes, Keith," Robin chimed in, trying to get on my good side. "I think that's a good idea."

*I swear, that bitch just don't know.*

"Okay, why not. Hire us a maid, shawty." Keith picked Robin up and carried her upstairs with him.

Well, I can't say that him taking her upstairs didn't bother me because it did and not because of jealousy or personal feelings. I guess it was a matter of Keith preferring her over me most of the time.

I was happy that Keith had agreed that I could hire a maid. I couldn't wait to call Momma in the morning to let her know. Honey, you talking about *Guess Who's Coming to Dinner.* How about, "Guess who's cooking dinner?"

# Chapter 20

Today was the day Momma was to come by in full disguise and meet the one big happy family. The only thing Keith didn't want the maid to know was that he swung both ways. So, Robin was to play his wife, and I was to play her cousin from California. Whateva.

Anyway, Momma was going to be Ms. Annabelle Stewart from Columbia, South Carolina, and she had been staying here in Omaha for the past eleven years taking care of her son and his family. Chile, I was hoping I could remember all this shit. Anywho, I had asked Keith and Robin to be here at the house by five p.m. because Ms. Stewart would be stopping by to formally meet them.

The three of us sat in the living room drinking a glass of wine and chitchatting while waiting on Momma. Of course, I didn't have much to say. I was so nervous, I kept looking at the clock on the wall every two seconds.

Suddenly, the intercom buzzed, and I almost peed on myself. I pressed the button to open the gate because I knew it wasn't anyone else but Momma.

"That must be Ms. Stewart," I said, trying to sound

cheerful. I got up and answered the front door.

Chile, I opened the door, and my mouth fell open. The woman that stood in front of me looked nothing like my mother. She had on this old, tired, gray-ass wig, which looked like she had it on backwards, and a brown plaid church mother dress. And to top things off, she had on these black orthopedic quarter inch-heel shoes. I swear, Momma looked like she was every bit of sixty years old.

She first looked at me, smiling and winking. She said with a strong Southern drawl, "Hello, Mr. Jenkins. It's so nice seeing you again."

"Same here, Ms. Stewart." I let her in, trying my best not to laugh. "Ms. Stewart, let me introduce you to my cousin Robin and her husband Keith."

"It's nice to finally meet you, Ms. Stewart," they both said in unison.

"Aw, it's so nice to meet you young chirren, but y'all don't have to call me Ms. Stewart. Just call me Momma. That's what e'rybody calls me, yup."

I invited Momma to have a seat on the couch and offered her something to drink as well.

"Yes, baby, I'd like to have a glass of ice cold water if ya got it. Now, you don't half to go ta no trouble on my account, but when you get my age, ya have ta make sho all ya fluids are running. So, I drink water e'ry chance I get, you know. Well, I guess you young'uns don't know. Oh well."

I went to the kitchen to get Momma some ice water and was cracking up. Momma was putting on a true performance. I couldn't believe it was her. If she could fool me, I knew she could fool Robin as well.

I got back into the living room with Momma's water.

Keith asked, "Ms. Stewart…I mean, Momma, how old are you?"

"I'm sixty-two years young, baby."

"Well, don't you think you're a lil too old?" he asked.

"Hell naw, baby. I'm as lively as they come. You wanna

**174**

race out to da gate?" Momma asked in a serious tone, standing up and challenging Keith.

One hour or so into our conversation, Momma had us cracking up, easily winning Keith and Robin over with her wit, Southern accent, and sense of humor.

But then Robin said, "Momma, I don't mean to stare at you, but you look so familiar."

I became so nervous. I dropped my wineglass right on the floor.

Everyone looked at me, including Momma, who gave me the look that said everything was gonna be all right.

"Aw, baby, peoples tells me that all the time. I'm always looking like somebody's grandmother, aunt, or neighbor dat lives up da street or someting," Mommy said, putting the focus back on her while I cleaned up my mess.

"Yeah, I guess you're right," Robin said.

Keith got up to refresh his cocktail. "Momma, would you like to have something a little stronger than that water you been drinking?"

"Well, I don't usually drink, but e'ry now and 'gain I will take a little taste, you know for my rheumatism," she replied, rubbing her leg.

"Would you like some wine?" Keith asked.

"That would be nice, but I see you got some gin over dere too."

"Ooo, I'm scared of you." Keith laughed. "Gin on the rocks coming up."

"Naw, baby, I ain't said nuf'n 'bout no ice." Momma turned and looked at him. "Did you hear me say *ice*?"

"Straight gin it is." Keith chuckled. "So, Momma, when can you start?"

"Well, first, lemme say I can only work Mondays, Wednesdays, and Fridays, from nine a.m. to three p.m., 'cause I gotta watch *Oprah*. She comes on at four p.m. You know dat, right?"

Keith handed Momma her drink.

"Dang, Momma!" Robin said, pouting. "Don't seem as though I will get a chance to see much of you because those are the days I'm in class."

"Don't you frit none, baby girl. You's get dat edumacation." Momma looked at me. "Edumacation comes in pretty handy in dese here times."

Robin sucked her teeth. "Ain't that the truth."

Time was going by so fast that before anybody knew it, it was almost eleven p.m. Momma said good night to everyone, gave us all a hug and kiss, and left.

I wanted to know what Robin and Keith really thought of Momma. "Well, what do you guys think?"

Interestingly enough, they both loved her. I was glad to hear that because now I could have her here and spend more time with her without raising suspicion. Also, I wasn't sure all of what Momma had planned, but I did what she asked, and that was to get her in the house.

*

You know, every now and then, I would still wake up in a cold sweat, dreaming about Ray, and seeing that guy that Keith had shot in the face and his blood gushing out onto me.

Tonight was one of those nights. I looked over on my dresser, and the clock read 2:45 a.m. I tossed and turned but couldn't go back to sleep. I sat up in my bed and wanted to call someone just to talk, but I didn't have anybody to call. I was feeling so lonely.

I then remembered the guy I had met at the filling station while I was getting some gas a few months ago.

"Dayum! What was his name?" I said to myself.

I jumped out of bed to see if I still had his number in my bag. I threw everything in my bag out on my bed, and there was his card. "Zachary Davis, that was his name," I said to myself.

*Would it be right to call someone this time of morning?* I thought. I sat back up in the bed, grabbed my cell, and dialed the number. Someone picked up on the fourth ring.

**176**

"Hello," a groggy voice said.

"Umm, can I speak to Zachary, please?" I asked, feeling bad for calling so late.

"Speaking. Who is this?"

"Umm, this is Cameron. I met you a few months ago at the BP gas station up on Crane Highway." I bit my bottom lip, hoping he would remember me.

"Yeah, I think so. You're the light-skin shawty with the braids, right?"

"Yeah," I said, feeling good about him remembering who I was. "Well, I had braids, but I've since taken them out of my hair. Now my hair is kinda short."

Zack cleared his throat. "What time is it?"

"I'm sorry. It is kinda late."

"Naw, shawty, it's cool. I was just wondering what time it was."

"It's after three in the morning. I was up and couldn't go to sleep," I stated, trying to start a conversation.

"That's cool. So, why can't you sleep?" he said in his now sexy voice.

"It's kind of a long story, and I'm sure you're not really interested."

"Sure, I am. It's Saturday morning and I'm off, so tell me."

I told Zachary, or Z, as he preferred to be called, the story about my older brother being murdered almost five years ago. I didn't bother to go into all the gory details, nor did I tell him about my current situation with Keith. I didn't want to turn the guy completely off.

But we talked for hours. I learned that he and his lover broke up a couple of years ago. He was thirty-three years of age and a Libran, planet Venus, goddess of love, and he loved being a lawyer. He also told me his parents were aware of his sexual preference and were fine with it. They actually loved his former lover and used to call him their son as well.

It had been so long since I had just talked to another guy.

You know what I mean? And it felt so dayum good. There was nothing sexual about our conversation, but I was totally turned on.

Z had invited me over his house later this evening for dinner and to watch a movie. We eventually hung up as the morning sun came shining through my bedroom blinds. I tossed and turned but still couldn't go to sleep. Fortunately, this time, it was because of my excitement and not my loneliness. I couldn't wait to see Z.

*

That evening I pulled up to the address Z had given me. Omaha can be somewhat confusing because it has a lot of small suburban areas, but this was the exact address. I questioned it only because it was in a very poor area of town, and Z being a lawyer, I thought perhaps he would be living in a better neighborhood.

*Well, maybe he isn't a very good lawyer.*

Anyway, it wasn't about material possessions. This was about meeting a new friend and spending time with that person. So I parked the car, looked into my rearview mirror, making sure I didn't put too much foundation on and that my hair was in place. I was nervous and excited all at the same time.

I didn't know what Z was going to make for dinner, but I did bring a bottle of white wine just for the occasion. I grabbed the wine that I placed in the passenger seat and made my way up the few steps to the front door.

The house was a traditional-style two-story house. The roof looked to be in bad shape because some of the shingles had fallen onto the porch. The house was painted in a gray OD-type color, and the windows were outlined in a dark purple color.

*Ewww,* I thought to myself as I stood there ringing the doorbell. The house was attached to a house on either side. The windows of the house on the left were open, and I picked up a smell, as though someone was trying to cook, but whatever it was, it smelled awful. And in the house on the right, it sounded as though some woman was beating and cussing out her small child. I felt sorry for the child because she/he was screaming their asses off.

*Come on, Z, answer this dayum door.*

After ringing the doorbell a few times and knocking on the door, I was becoming disappointed, feeling as though I had been stood up.

Just as I was walking down the steps to get in my car to leave, *Z* pulled up and got out of his car.

"Hey, Cameron, I'm so sorry. I had to stop at the store to pick up a couple of things at the last minute. I should have known a brotha like you would be on time." He started getting some grocery bags out of his car.

"Oh, it's cool. Would you like some help with the bags?"

"Naw, I got it." *Z* opened the door for me. "Come on in."

I entered into his place, and to be honest, the inside didn't look any better. Now, I was truly not a bogey type of person, although I couldn't help that I had good taste. But as I looked around at *Z*'s home, I started to wonder why they hadn't condemned this place before it fell on its own. It appeared to only be standing on a wing and a prayer anyhow.

*Z* put his groceries away and took me on a tour of his home. He did tell me that he only bought this property as an investment and that he was actually in the process of fixing it up. All I can say was, the tour didn't last long because each room looked as bad as the other.

I told him how hungry I was, and he took me down to his kitchen and began fixing me a plate. I had to give the brotha credit because he was buying real estate and fixing them up. Donald Trump did it all the time. So, who's to say that in a few years Mr. Zachary Davis won't be this big-time mogul?

Anyways, *Z* fixed my plate, and we sat down to eat. What surprised me was, before eating, *Z* wanted to hold hands and say grace. That really impressed me, a spiritual brotha. However, the food wasn't that great. He cooked some kind of baked fish, baked potatoes, and fresh broccoli, all half-cooked. *Z* noticed I was having a hard time eating my food and apologized profusely, but I told him it was okay, it was the thought that count.

Later, we sat in his half-decorated living room and watch this movie called, *Torch Song Trilogy*, which he said was one of his favorite movies. I had never heard of the movie, but I really, really enjoyed it. It was about this gay white dude who performed in drag and was looking for love and a family to call his own. Very emotional movie. Had me crying and shit. I was so embarrassed, but Z told me not to be because when he first saw it, it made him cry as well. That made me feel a lot better.

Unfortunately, I wasn't that attracted to Z physically because he was tall, really tall, and rather thin. Of course, I've heard about those tall, thin brothas with the big dicks. Yes! But what I did like about Z was his personality. He was sweet, caring, affectionate, and attentive. He catered to me to make sure I was comfortable, or whether or not I wanted more to drink. He held my hand as we watched the movie. All the things that a girl would love, you know.

I wasn't planning on sleeping with him, at least not on the first date. *But could he hit this? Absolutely.*

At about midnight, Z walked me to my car and gave me a nice warm hug. I was surprised, considering it was outside. Granted, no one was out that time of night, but I was still surprised he would do that so openly. You know how some guys will fuck you silly and everything else behind closed doors, but as soon as you get them out in public, half the time they act like they don't know you. But I gave Z big points for that because that's all I needed, was just a warm hug, and it was perfect.

\*

The whole drive home, I thought about Z and how good he made me feel. We had made plans for later that day to actually go to a movie. He told me that since I sat and watched his movie, I could pick any movie and we would go check it out, his treat. He actually started giving me butterflies. I felt like some schoolgirl.

I made it to the mansion and drove up to the gate and input my code. The gate opened, and I pulled right in the driveway. It appeared as though no one was home, because all the lights were out.

"Good," I said to myself.

As soon as I entered the front foyer, I was slapped so hard in the face, I fell to the floor.

Suddenly, the lights came on, and standing over top of me was Keith. "Where the fuck did you go?" he yelled, looking down at me.

I held the side of my face and tried to get the ringing out of my ear. "Why did you do that, Keith?"

He yelled, "I asked you a simple question! Don't have me ask you again!"

"I-I-I went out with with my sister Keisha," I replied trying to get up.

"Don't fuckin' lie to me, dammit!" Keith slapped me once again and knocked me back down to the floor.

I cried out, curling myself up in a ball. "I-I-I ain't lying."

"What? You think I'm stupid?" he screamed, still standing over top of me. "You think I don't know your every fuckin' move?"

"What do you want from me?" I blabbed, hiding my face with my hands.

"You belong to me, you hear me? I betta not ever see you with that dude again. What? You don't think I know who he is? Mr. Zachary Davis. I know that punk-ass muthafucka, too. Stand yo' ass up!" He grabbed me by my shirt.

Chile, I didn't know how Keith knew about Z. I could only assume that he must have been following me and I wasn't aware of it.

I stood up in tears as Keith slammed my body against the wall. "If I ever see you with anybody else, their ass is mine, and yours is, too!" he yelled in my face, "And don't you forget that shit! Now, take your ass to your room, take a shower, and get ready fo' dis dick!"

As I walked up the stairs, holding the side of my face, I passed by Robin, who was just standing there with a big-ass grin on her face. Obviously she'd been standing there the whole time.

I guess I couldn't blame her. *What could she say?*

This was the first time Keith had ever hit me and made these kinds of demands. It frightened me. So, I did what I was told. I took a hot shower and prepared myself for him.

# Chapter 21

I sat at the kitchen table Monday morning waiting for my Momma to arrive for her first day of work. I was on my third cup of coffee, thinking about my life. I had come to the conclusion that I didn't mind being gay. I just wished I wasn't as passive as I was, because some brothas took advantage of that. I'd been around and seen other bottom brothas out here that was as masculine as they come and didn't seem to have some of the same problems as the more feminine ones like me. Not to mention, these same masculine bottom brothas seemed to be able to get those hard, masculine top brothas more easily.

There seems to be a certain amount of prejudice among those masculine bottom brothas versus those feminine bottom brothas. I'm not sure why that is, considering we all like the very same thing.

I had this one masculine bottom brotha tell me once that he didn't like feminine bottom brothas because he didn't feel it was necessary to be so obvious. I told him that I had nothing to hide, and that obviously he was ashamed about who and what he was. Anyways, I wished there wasn't so much conspiracy between bottom brothas, regardless whether they were masculine or feminine because, the bottom line is, we all had a story to tell, and we all had to fight the same battle.

I didn't see *Z* yesterday, even though he'd called and texted me several times. Keith had made it very clear with his threat, so I didn't want *Z* to get caught up in my bullshit. I figured, once all this was over, I would call *Z* and explain everything. Until then, I had to keep my distance from him.

I felt like a caged animal, locked up and not able to have a relationship with anyone. But, as much as I began to despise Keith, I still enjoyed sex with him. But how could this be? My mind said no, but my body was aching for him.

*Buzz!*

I heard the intercom and jumped up to press the gate button so my Momma could enter. In a way, I felt like a little kid because I was going to spend time with her. I went and stood at the door and watched as Momma drove up and parked.

"Good morning, suga," she said, walking in with full disguise on.

I held the door open for her. "Good morning, Ms. Stewart…I mean, Momma," I replied, giving her a hug.

Keith came down the stairs and caught us both off guard. "Morning, Momma."

"Good morning, young man." Momma gave Keith a hug. "And where is the missus this fine morning?"

"She has classes early on Mondays, Wednesdays, and Fridays. She told you that, remember?"

"Oh that's right. I tell ya, my mind ain't what it used ta be, but boy, can I cook. Now, what you young'uns like ta have for breakfast?"

We headed out into the kitchen.

"Nothing for me, Momma. I don't eat breakfast. Besides, I have some errands to run. We hadn't gone shopping for food or anything, but Cameron here can take you and get whatever you need, a'ight" Keith stated grabbing a cup of coffee.

"Well, baby, don't you know that breakfast is the most important meal of the day?"

"I know, Momma. I'm just never up in time. You two have fun," Keith said as he walked out the kitchen.

"Whew! I didn't think his stupid ass would ever leave." Momma sat down at the table and pulled her wig off. "You know it's kind of hard smiling in his face and shit after you told me what he did to you."

"I know, Momma, and I love you for it. But, like you said, we got work to do." I put Momma's wig back on her head.

"Look, don't get cute. Now, where's this safe?" she asked, standing up.

After checking the house and making sure that both Keith and Robin were gone, I took Momma into Keith's office and opened the safe for her.

"Wow, baby!" Momma said, looking at the stacks of hundred-dollar bills. "We oughta take this money here and run."

I took all the money out and placed it on the coffee table. "I wonder how much it is."

"Give me a few, and I'll tell you. In the meantime keep an eye out at the door, just in case."

"I can do betta than that. Check this out," I said, pulling up all the cameras around the area, including the one at the front gate, on Keith's computer.

"Dayum! This muthafucka got it going on, huh." Momma laughed as she counted Keith's money.

"So he thinks." I looked at all the cameras on the computer screen. "So, Momma, when do you wanna take the money and leave?"

"Hmmm. I don't know. We might have to wait until the first of the month because this muthafucka here has records of all his pickups and drops." Momma's eyes grew bigger. "And according to his book here, on the first of next month, he should have over one million dollars in this safe."

"Wow! Are you serious?" A lump started forming in my throat.

"Yeah, baby. Momma doesn't joke when it comes to

**185**

money. Ah, is there any way you can have Keith, Robin, and Junior here on the first of the month?" Momma was still looking through Keith's account booklet.

"I can have Keith and Robin, but like I said, Keith makes sure that Junior and I don't see one another. Why do you ask?"

"Baby, if we take his money, there's no way he will let us just run away with it. He will come looking, and once he finds us, he will kill us," Momma said in a serious tone.

"So, what are you saying?" I asked nervously. "You wanna kill them?"

"We have to, not only for the money, baby, but for Ray as well," she responded, looking me dead in the eyes.

"Momma, I don't know…I'm scared." I got up and started pacing the floor.

"I know you're scared, Cameron. And please don't take this the wrong way, but I need you to man up, all right." She put her hands on my shoulders. "Now, listen to me. There is almost two hundred fifty thousand dollars lying over there on that table. If we take it, he will surely come after us, but if we hold out and plan, we can get four times that amount and not have to worry about looking over our shoulders."

"How we gonna do that, Momma?"

"Don't worry about that, baby. Just have them here on the first, and I'll take care of everything else. In the meantime, let's put this money away, turn off that computer, and get out of here."

My mom and I put everything back the way it was and headed out to the grocery store to pick up some food for the house. Once we got to the grocery, I grabbed a cart and started thinking back to whether or not my mother could actually cook.

"So, Momma, can you cook?" I asked, speeding up and walking by her down the frozen meat aisle.

"Hell, yes, I can cook. Actually, I'm a very good cook, for your information."

"Hmmm. So, what's for dinner? Steak?" I grinned.

Momma put the cube beef steak in the cart. "Smart ass."

"So, we meet again," a familiar voice stated behind me. I turned around. "Oh! Hey, *Z*. How are you?"

"And who is this, baby?" Momma asked, smiling all in *Z*'s face.

"I'm sorry. *Z*, this is my…I mean, this is Ms. Stewart. Ms. Stewart, this is Zachary Davis."

"It's very nice to meet you, Mr. Davis." Momma smiled and held up the back of her hand to be kissed.

*Z* kissed Momma's hand. "The pleasure is all mine, Ms. Stewart."

"Oh dear boy, no need to be formal. Just call me Annabelle," Momma said, flirting.

I cleared my throat. "So, how you been, *Z*?"

"I've been good. A little disappointed that you never returned my call," he said, looking me dead in the eye.

"Well, I guess I'll let you young people talk. I got a lot of groceries to get. It's been real nice meeting you, Mr. Davis," Momma said as she walked away.

"Why did you stand me up?"

"Umm, something came up, and I got busy. I was gonna call you, but I thought you would be upset." I bit my bottom lip.

"You got busy and you were gonna call, but you thought I would be upset. Okay," he said, disappointment in his eyes.

"*Z*, you're a really nice guy, and I like you a lot, but there are things going on in my life right now that I really don't wanna get into, okay. Now, once this is over, I will call you, I promise," I said in a genuine tone.

"Yo, man, it's cool. If you ain't feeling me like that, why can't you just say so?"

"Because I'm feeling you. I just can't do anything about it right now. Please believe me. I will call you." I walked away from him.

\*

Momma and I had gotten all the groceries we needed to last us for the entire week. As we got into the car, of course, she wanted to know the story behind Mr. Davis. I explained to her that he was the guy I had had a date with on Saturday evening, and when I'd returned home, Keith slapped me a few times because he thought I was cheating on him.

Momma then got quiet.

I looked over at her and could see in her eyes that she was getting upset about Keith hitting on me.

"It's okay, Momma," I said, rubbing her hands.

"No, baby, it's not okay. A man ain't supposed to put his hands on you, period."

"I know, but I just don't like seeing you getting upset," I stated softly.

"He will pay. You can believe that, or my name ain't Ms. Annabelle Stewart!" She folded her arms around her chest.

"Momma, your name is Ms. Janet Wilson, or have you forgot?"

Momma looked at me and I looked at her, and we both burst out laughing.

After a minute or so and the laughter quieted down, Momma said she was just checking to see if I was paying attention.

*Yeah, right!*

Anywho, since we had a couple more weeks of this charade, Momma said she needed to stop by a thrift store so she could get a few more old lady dresses. Of course the thrift store, or Goodwill store, as some people called them, was not my kinda place to shop. But it didn't matter to me because I was spending time with my momma, and I was enjoying every second of it. I had never been to a Goodwill store, but I recalled seeing one at the Whitmore Shopping Center, which wasn't far from where I lived.

Within minutes, we were pulling into the shopping center and into a parking space rather close to the entrance.

Momma and I got out of the car and strutted arm in arm into the store. And, honey, I hadn't even made it that far into the store before the odor or musk from the old clothes almost knocked me out. I had to stand there for a minute just to get myself together.

Momma turned and looked at me. "What's wrong, baby?"

"What is that smell?" I asked, covering my nose.

Now, if I hadn't been there, I wouldn't have believed it, but Momma hit me upside my head and said, "Chile boo," and kept on walking.

Chile, I hollered. After she said that, for some reason, I couldn't smell the odor anymore. "No, you didn't," I said, catching up with her.

"Yes, I did." She started looking through a rack of old dresses.

As I stood next to her looking at one dress after another, there were a few odds and ends that caught my attention. I left my mom where she was and began looking at one thing, and then something else caught my attention, and before I knew it, I grabbed a cart, and within minutes, I had a cart full of shit.

Chile, I was like a kid in a candy store. Now, I understood why so many people shopped here. And they had these 1960s leopard tights that were in perfect shape and cost only two bucks. Humph, they mine now. On top of that, I saw this light blue boa they had wrapped around one of those plastic mannequins, and you know I had to have it.

Momma finally caught up with me, looked inside my cart and shook her head. "A boa?"

I looked back at her. "Yeah, and?"

"I don't even wanna know." She chuckled.

We made it back to the house, and Momma told me she was gonna show me how much of a great cook she was. We unpacked the bags and put all the food away.

She sat down at the table. "Have you thought of a way to have the three of them here on the first of the month?"

"Not yet. We just spoke about it earlier. I hadn't thought about it yet." I sat down at the table across from her.

"Well, Cameron, you should always be planning your next move, baby. Remember, you always gotta stay ahead of the enemy." She got up and poured herself a cup of coffee. "Would you like a cup?"

"No, Momma, I'm good. So, let me ask you. Have you thought of a way to get all of them here on the first?"

"As a matter fact, I have."

"Oh, really?"

"Well, I was thinking while we were in the grocery store, How about I throw a dinner party for them?"she stated, sitting back down at the kitchen table.

"A dinner party?" I asked with a raised eyebrow. "What's the occasion?"

"Hmmm. How about I play matchmaker?" She smiled.

"Matchmaker? Who are you matchmaking?"

"Well, let's say I have a gorgeous granddaughter that I wanna hook up with Junior?" She sipped her coffee.

"Whatchoo talking about, Momma?"

"How about the next time I see Keith, I start asking him questions about his family? If he tells me he has a brother and I get all the vital information, I'll then tell him about my gorgeous granddaughter and that I wanna have a dinner party so they can meet. How does that sound?"

I shook my head. "There's only one problem, Momma."

"And what's that, darling?"

"Ah, you don't have a granddaughter. Duh!"

"I know that, and you know that, but they don't know that." She winked at me as she sipped her coffee.

"So, what happens when they show up and this gorgeous granddaughter doesn't?"

"Baby, I just wanna get them all in one place. And the least of their worry will be my granddaughter," Momma said with a devilish grin. "Trust me."

# Chapter 22

After a few weeks, Momma had Keith and Robin just where she wanted them. They'd actually started treating her as though she was their real momma.Whenever Keith mistreated Robin, she would go to Momma seeking advice and shit. I thought it was the funniest thing, because Momma would tell her to do shit that made no sense, but stupid-ass Robin would do it anyway. Which would cause Keith to be even more upset.

Keith wasn't any better, calling Momma at home and complaining about Robin did this and Robin did that. Stupid muthafuckas, they all had what was coming to them.

When Momma first asked Keith about the dinner party and wanting to set her granddaughter up with his brother, Keith originally said he would pass on the idea, but by the time Momma finished babying him and catering to him, a week later he changed his mind. Told Momma he couldn't wait to meet her granddaughter, and besides, his little brother needed to meet someone and settle down.

When Momma told me that, I fell out. Momma also said that Keith said he had an appointment scheduled for that same evening and that he had to be there by eleven p.m. Momma said she assured him that the dinner party would be over no later than ten p.m.

And as luck would have it, I didn't have to make up some lame excuse for not being present because Keith actually lied to Momma and said his brother didn't like homosexuals, that he didn't know if Momma noticed but I was one flaming queen, and if she could talk me into making other plans so I wouldn't be there.

Ain't that some shit? Flaming queen. The nerve. He don't be saying that shit when he be dicking me down, the faggot-ass muthafucka. But little did he know, I was gonna be making my grand appearance, okay.

Anyways, a few days before the dinner party, Momma said she wanted to visit my stepfather, Mr. William Jenkins, and get his ass straight about his threats towards me and my sister. And she also wanted to go see Ms. Gerdy and thank her for what she had done for raising her kids and to say good-bye.

\*

"Well, Momma, what are you planning on saying to him?" I asked her on the drive headed towards my stepfather's grocery store.

"I'ma give his ass a piece of my mind," she said, her lips poked out.

"Momma, he doesn't even know who you are. Why would he care what you say? Besides, am I to introduce you to him as my mother or Ms. Stewart?" I looked at Momma out of the corner of my eye. She was still in her Ms. Stewart disguise.

"Suga, it really doesn't matter at this point." She opened her purse and showed me what looked like a gun.

"Momma, where did you get that from?"

"Don't worry, baby. Momma, got this." She sat back in the seat and twisted her neck from side to side.

"You not gonna shoot him, are you?"

"That depends." Momma shrugged her shoulders.

"Depends on what?"

"Depends on whether he wants to keep on living, baby," she said, looking at me.

My eyes popped out as I continued to drive, and a lump got caught in my throat. I tried hard to swallow, but the thoughts that ran in and out of my head were making it hard to do so. I didn't know what Momma was going to say to my stepfather, and worse yet, I didn't know if she was actually going there to kill this man or not. Either way, I didn't have a good feeling about this.

I began thinking that may be Momma had spent too much time in that sanitarium and just might be crazy.

*

I found a parking space right out front of my stepfather's store. I parked the car, and Momma and I got out and headed into the store.

"Hi, Cameron," Ms. Ruby stated. "Haven't seen you around here in a while. How have you been?"

"I'm good, Ms. Ruby. I just stopped by because I wanted to see my father. Is he in?"

"Yeah, he's back there in his office. Why don't you go on back there and surprise him?"

"I think I will. Thanks."

Momma and I headed towards the back, where my step-father's office was located. His office door was closed, so I knocked.

"What are you doing?" Momma asked me.

"Knocking on the door."

"Boy, please." Momma opened his door.

I walked in first with Momma right behind me. My step-father was sitting at his desk looking at some reports and still hadn't noticed us standing there.

Momma cleared her throat.

"Hey, Dad," I said as nice as I could.

"What da hell?" He raised his head and noticed that I

wasn't by myself.

"Dad, this is…"

"Janet, is that you?" He put on his glasses that were on his desk and stood up.

Momma slammed his office door. "In the flesh, Bill."

"Wha-wha-what are you doing here?"

"Are you gonna invite us to have a seat, Bill?" Momma asked, standing there with her hands on her hips.

I didn't know what was going on, but whatever it was, Momma and my stepfather knew each other, and he seemed a little scared of her.

"Ah, ah, sure. Have a seat." He too sat back down and started shifting around in his seat.

"Don't worry, Bill. No need to be nervous. I didn't call the po-po on yo' trifling ass." Momma said sitting down.

"Look, Janet, before…"

"No, Bill, you look. I'm here because I don't like any-one…do you hear me, Bill? I don't like anyone threatening my kids, and according to Cameron, you threatened him and Keisha. Is that true, Bill?" Momma pulled out her gun and twirled it around her fingers.

Chile, I felt like I was at a dayum movie or something. Momma wasn't taking shit from this man, a man who had bullied me as well as Ms. Gerdy. And now to see him act like a bitch in front of Momma was freaking me out. What did Momma have on this man?

"Yo, sis, you know I wouldn't harm my own kin folk. Hell, I was just playing with the boy. I wouldn't do such a thing."

"Sis?" I looked at Momma then at my stepfather.

"Yeah, baby, this is Bill, my older brother…your uncle," Momma said, looking at me. "So, now that the introductions been made, I need you to apologize to your nephew." Momma stood up and walked to the back of my uncle's chair.

"Come on, Janet. I was just having a little fun with the boy. I wasn't gonna hurt him."

"Cameron, did I ever tell you the time when my brother, your uncle here…" Momma pointed the gun at his head, "blew up our parents' house with them in it, just so he could collect on their life insurance policy? And you sit here and say, he kinfolk and you wouldn't have hurt him?" Momma hit him over the head with the butt of the gun.

My uncle held the back of his head. "Ouch! Shit!"

"Now, Bill, like I said, you need to apologize to your nephew. Or how 'bout I tell Gerdy that you just married her so that you could kill her and collect on her insurance policy as well? Or how about I just call the po-po and let them know you were responsible for killing one of their own? When was this, Bill, six or seven years ago when you came running to my house and cried like a little bitch because you thought the po-po was gonna catch yo' punk ass because you didn't wanna go to prison?" Momma circled him like a vulture.

"I apologize," he stated softly, still holding the back of his head.

"Speak up, muthafucka! I couldn't hear that shit. Did you, Cameron?" Momma looked over at me.

I laughed. "No, ma'am."

"I apologize," he replied, almost yelling.

"Now, was that so hard? And the next time I hear anything about you threatening my kids, I will kill you."Momma took her seat and put her gun back in her purse.

I guess that was a good thing because at that point Ms. Ruby opened the office door.

"Everything all right?"she asked.

Uncle Bill responded, "Yeah, Ruby, everything is fine."

"Okay, I was just checking." She closed the door.

"So, you knew you were my uncle? Why did you treat me that way?"

"Baby, he treated you that way because as a gay bottom man himself, he has a problem with feminine gay individuals. I think deep down inside, he wish he could be more like you, but he's too dayum scared. Scared of what society might think. So he overcompensate by butching it up, even though you love yourself some dick too. Or don't you remember telling me that when we were younger? Ain't that right, Bill?"

Uncle Bill never said a word. He just hung his head low, looking down at his desk.

I wanted to feel sorry for him, but how could I?

"Well, baby, it's time for us to leave. I've said my piece." Momma got up and opened the office door.

We walked out to the front of the store, where I saw Ms. Ruby waiting on a customer.

"See you, Ms. Ruby. Have a nice day," I said, as Momma and I walked out of the store.

Momma and I got in the car, looked at one another, and cracked up. Momma was something else.

"Now, I wanna go see Gerdy," she said, putting on her seat belt.

"Okay, Momma. But, wow, I can't get over the fact that you and the man I knew as my stepfather are brother and sister. Why didn't you tell me before now?"

"Baby, you find out things in life all in good time."

"But you said you didn't have any family. I knew that your parents had died in a fire, but I didn't know it was because of Uncle Bill."

"So, now you know."

"So, Momma, had you thought about where we would go after the dinner party?"

"I sure have."

"Where?"

"I've always wanted to go to New York. Even as a child, I thought that someday I would go there but never had a chance. Now I do, and I can hardly wait."

"Why New York, Momma?"

"It's the city that never sleeps, baby. Not like tired-ass Omaha, you know. I wanna walk through Times Square. I wanna see the Statue of Liberty in person. Let's just say, I wanna take a bite out of The Big Apple." Momma laughed.

Minutes later, we pulled up in front of Ms. Gerdy's house. This time I parked in the driveway because I no longer feared my uncle. I was with Momma, so he knew better than to fuck with me ever again.

We got out of the car and walked up to the front door.

"Do you want me to introduce you as Momma or Ms. Annabelle Stewart?"

"Let's see if she recognizes me first," Momma said, ringing the doorbell.

"Wait a minute!" I heard Ms. Gerdy yell.

"She must be cooking because I smell something that sure smells good," Momma said.

"Well, Cameron, why are you ringing the doorbell?" Ms. Gerdy asked as she opened the door.

"Hey, Ma," I said as we walked in. I gave her a hug. "I brought a friend of mine by for you to meet. "Ma, this is Ms. Stewart. Ms. Stewart, this is Ma."

"It's nice to meet you, Ms. Stewart. Y'all come on out in the kitchen 'cause I got food on the stove." Ma led us out into her kitchen.

"Same here. You have a lovely home," Momma said as we entered the kitchen.

Ma took a closer look at Momma. "Janet?"

"Yeah, girl. How have you been?" Momma gave Ma a big ol' hug.

"Well, lawd, Janet Wilson, as I live and breathe." Ma looked at Momma up and down. "Well, what…I mean when…what do you have on, honey chile?"

"I know I look older than you, but I'm going to a little get-together and we're supposed to dress up like an old person. So, don't even go there. You know I'm still all that." Momma took off her wig and straightened out her jazzy bob hairdo.

"Well, you surprised me. Cameron, you didn't tell me your mother was out," Ma said, looking at me.

"I know, Ma, but Momma asked me not to say anything

**197**

because she wanted to surprise you."

"Well, y'all sure did that. Why don't y'all have a seat? Y'all hungry? I can fix y'all a plate. And I know you hungry, Cameron. You just so thin, sweetie."

"Ma, I'm thin because I wanna be. I have to watch my figure," I said, laughing.

"Janet, that child of yours, I swear..."

"I know, Gerdy. You ain't gotta tell me. And, yes, I would love a plate. Everything just smells so good."

We all sat and talked for hours. I watched Ma and Momma go back and forth talking about the good ol' days and how they used to go out from time to time. Ma told Momma that she remarried and how much she loved her husband, but the interesting thing was that Momma never told Ma that her husband was her brother. I definitely had to ask Momma about that later.

But I enjoyed watching them talk, and laugh until they cried. I truly loved these two women, one very meek and mild, the other strong and aggressive.

"Well, Gerdy, before we leave, I seriously just wanna thank you for what you did for my kids. I thank you and love you for doing that." Momma had tears in her eyes as she looked at Ms. Gerdy.

"Janet, I should be thanking you. Your kids have brought so much joy in my life, and for that, I've been blessed. Thank you." Ma got up and hugged Momma.

"Y'all need to stop that because y'all gonna make me cry too." I got up and hugged them both.

"And, Gerdy, I need one last favor."Momma sat back down at the table.

"What, Janet? What's wrong?"

"Everything is fine, Gerdy, but like I said, Keshia has been staying with me. This Saturday, I want her to stay here with you, and I will pick her up on Sunday. Is that okay with you?"

"Sure, baby. That's not a problem at all. This is still Keisha's home, just like it's still Cameron's home." Ma smiled at me.

"Thank you, Gerdy," Mommy said in a genuine tone.

"Look, Janet, you gonna have to stop all this thanking-me stuff. These kids have been calling me Ma for the past almost five years. Now stop it, you hear me?"

"Okay, Gerdy, I just love you for what you've done for my kids. I can't help but say thank you."

"Okay, Janet. You're welcome," Ma replied, looking at Momma with her head hanging down. "Hey, maybe you can do the same for me one day." Ma laughed while holding Momma's chin up with her hand.

And with that, Ma and Momma were back at laughing and talking about the good ol' times once again.

# Chapter 23

Today was Saturday the first, the day when all the shit was gonna hit the fan, as Momma would say. It was high noon when I picked up Momma and Keisha, and then dropped Keisha off at Ms. Gerdy's house.

"Momma, why can't I come to the dinner party with you and Cameron?" Keisha pouted.

"Look, Keshia, it's for adults, okay. I promised we will hang out tomorrow, maybe go to the mall and do some shopping." Momma kissed her on the forehead.

"What time you gonna pick me up?"

"What time you want me to pick you up?" Momma smiled.

"Ah, eight o'clock."

"Girl, the mall don't open until ten a.m. Why eight o'clock?"

"We can stop at Micky Dee's for breakfast."

"Hmmm. Okay, okay. Love you. Mean it."

"Love you too, Momma," Keisha said, getting out of the car.

"Hey, what about me, little girl?" I pouted.

"Love you, too, Cameron." She was smiling and waving at me as she walked up on Ma's front porch.

We headed back to the mansion because Momma said Uncle Bill was stopping by to do her a favor and that he was supposed to be there by one p.m. I didn't know what kind of favor, and I didn't bother to ask. I knew Robin had left out earlier this morning to get her hair done, and a pedicure and manicure, as well as pick out a new outfit for tonight's dinner party, so I knew she would be gone most of the day. Keith on the other hand was to pick up Junior and have him back at the mansion by six forty-five p.m. because dinner would begin promptly at seven p.m.

Momma had gone all out by buying a black-and-white maid's outfit, along with one of those little white hats that maids used to wear back in the day. We went grocery shopping yesterday and purchased all that Momma had on her list like lunch meats, a variety of cheeses, Ritz Crackers for hors d'oeuvre, a variety of fruit, whipped cream, honey ham, a roast, turkey, yams, white potatoes, rice, stuffing, biscuit mix, and cake mix. You name it, Momma got it, along with red and white dinner wine.

Fortunately, Momma cooked most of the food last night, so today it was just a matter of warming most of it up.

Momma and I pulled up at the gate just in time because Uncle Bill had pulled up right behind us. I input the code and waved him to go around me so he could enter first. I then re-entered the code and proceeded through.

As we all got out of our cars, I noticed that Uncle Bill had a large black cloth bag that he carried over his shoulder. "What's that for?" I asked, looking at Momma and then at Uncle Bill.

"Don't worry about that, baby. Let's just let Uncle Bill here do his job, okay," Momma said as we entered the kitchen area.

"Where do you want me to begin?" Uncle Bill asked.

Momma told me, "Baby, why don't you go check and make sure no one else is here, all right."

"Okay, Momma. But no one's car is here but mine, so I know we are alone."

"Go check anyway," Momma snapped.

"Okay, okay," I replied going up the back kitchen stairwell.

I first checked Keith's room, and just as I thought, it was empty. Then I went to Robin's room, and her room was empty too. I then ran down the front stairs and checked Keith's office, and again, it was empty as well.

I walked back towards the kitchen and overheard Uncle Bill telling Momma, "Once I'm finished, don't ever contact me again, and my debt has been paid in full."

"Don't worry, you won't," Momma said with attitude, hands on her hips and her head twisting from side to side.

"We're the only ones here," I stated, interrupting their conversation.

"Good." Momma looked at Uncle Bill. "Now, you can go do what you do best."

Uncle Bill opened the black bag and pulled out two sets of headphones and began explaining to Momma and me how they worked. Uncle Bill then went to do his job, whatever that was, and Momma and I began testing the headphones. They weren't actually headphones per se, but they were very small devices that you place in your ear and the mic was a small round object that you attached to your clothing.

Momma put hers inside her bra, and I placed mine inside my high collar shirt. I then went from room to room testing the mic and earphone, and I could hear Momma as clear as if she was standing right in front of me.

I kept asking her, "Can you hear me now? Can you hear me now? like they do on the commercials, but Momma didn't think it was funny.

"Boy, cut that shit out and meet me in Keith's office."

I met Momma in Keith's office, and I knew exactly why

she wanted me to meet her there.

"The money and drugs should be in there, so go ahead, baby, and open up the safe for Momma," she stated, smiling from ear to ear.

"Well, Momma, if we get the money and stuff now, what if Keith decides to come home early and wants to go in the safe looking for something and sees that everything is gone?"

"Baby, don't worry about Keith. I will keep his drinking glass full. He will be so out of it, he won't know if he's coming or going, you hear me?"

I opened the safe, and just as Momma had predicted, based on Keith's figures in his book, there was a little over a million dollars in his safe.

Momma kept throwing the money up in the air talking about, "Come to Momma," and bursting out with laughter.

I sat there amazed at all the money in front of me. My mind was so overwhelmed, I couldn't think straight.

"Wow, Momma! We can live anywhere we want with all this money," I said, excitement in my voice.

"That's right, baby. And New York, here we come." Momma started placing the money in a black plastic trash bag.

After we loaded the money and the cocaine into the trash bag, Momma instructed me to go and place it in the trunk of my car and to make sure I put it under the trunk mat where the spare tire usually goes. Once I had done that, I met her back in the kitchen, where she had begun to take the dinner out of the refrigerator to warm up.

"Okay, Momma, it's in the trunk. Now what do you want me to do?" I sat down at the kitchen table and watched her every move.

"Well, baby, once your Uncle Bill leaves, I want you to drive your car up the road and park it behind the Waffle House. You can then walk back down here. That way, your Uncle Bill doesn't see it, and neither will Keith. And once our job here is done, all we have to do is walk up the road, get in the car and start our new life!" She was busy placing all the food on the table, looking as though she was trying to figure out what to warm up first.

"Momma, I'm nervous about this whole thing."

"Don't be. Don't you wanna get back at the bastard that killed your brother?"

"Yes, ma'am."

"And don't you wanna get back at that bitch for taking your man?"

"Yes, ma'am."

"And don't you wanna get back at that muthafucka for treating you the way he does?"

"Yes, ma'am."

"Well, then just do what I tell you to do and leave the rest up to Momma." She winked at me.

"Okay, Janet, I'm done," Uncle Bill stated. "Everything is set, so all you have to do is flip the living room switch."

"Fine. Have a good life, and good-bye," Momma said, her hands on her hips and twisting her neck.

"Dang, Momma! You twist your neck more than I do." I burst out laughing.

"Boy, hush and see your uncle to the door."

"Yes, ma'am."

I led Uncle Bill to the front door and watched him get in his car. He didn't say anything to me, but it was weird how he kept shaking his head as though he felt sorry for something. I had hoped it was because of the way he had been treating me, knowing damn well I was his nephew. *The muthafucka.*

I watched him drive out of the gate and down the road. I then hopped in my car and tried to drive to the Waffle House, but halfway there, the trunk popped open.

*Dayum! I must have not closed the trunk all the way.*

I couldn't stop so I continued to drive and I parked in the rear as Momma told me to.Once I got out of the car, I went to the trunk and noticed that the lock had been popped. I searched under the trunk mat, and the trash bag was nowhere to be found.

I began to get nauseous as though I was about to throw

up. "No, that muthafucka didn't!" I said out loud.

I got back in my car and went searching for Uncle Bill. There was no way I could go back home and tell Momma that the money and drugs were gone and that he had taken it. I was gonna demand that he give it all back to me, and if he tried anything, I would get Momma to kick his ass.

I went as fast as I could down the highway to his store because I knew he wouldn't take it home to Momma Gerdy's house.

Once I got to the store, I was informed that he hadn't been there all day and that he wouldn't be back until Monday.

I raced over to Momma Gerdy's house just to see if she had heard from him, and unfortunately she hadn't.

"Sweetie, what's wrong?" Momma Gerdy asked. "You look so pale. Are you hungry?"

"Naw, Ma, I'm not hungry. I'm just not feeling well." I sat down on the living room couch.

"What's going on? Why are you looking for your dad?"

"I just need to find him, Ma.Do you know where he can be?" I asked; my face in my hands.

"Did you check down at the store, sweetie? He should be there."

"Yes, Ma. I went there first."

"Hey, Cameron," Keisha said, coming down the stairs.

"Hey, baby sis," I replied, trying not to hyperventilate.

"Dang, Cam! What's wrong with you?" Keisha sat down on the couch next to me.

"I'm fine. I'll be all right," I spat raising my voice.

"Well excuse me," she responded as she got up and went into the kitchen.

"Sweetie, you sure you're okay?" Ma sat next to me and held my hand. "Is there anything you want me to do?"

"Naw, Ma, I'll be okay. I just need to find Uncle…I mean, Dad."

"Well, sweetie, it's Saturday. He might be over at the lodge, or he could be down at the church. Did you try there?"

"Naw, I didn't, and it would be just like him to go to the church of all places." I got up and headed for the front door.

"Sweetie, what do you mean, of all places? What happened? What did he do?"

"Ma, I can't explain now. I just need to find him. I will call you later and explain everything, okay." I walked out the door and towards my car.

*

Three hours or so had gone by, and I still hadn't found Uncle Bill. I stopped at the church and the lodge, but no one had seen him. It was a little after seven p.m., and I knew Keith, Robin, and Junior were all at the house. Momma was probably wondering where the hell I was. How could I go back there and tell Momma that Uncle Bill had taken the money and the drugs? The first time I was going to man up and demand back what Uncle Bill had taken, and I couldn't even find him. I had searched this whole city practically and couldn't find him or his car anywhere.

Having nowhere else to search or go, I headed back home to give Momma the bad news. I thought, *Maybe we could change our plans and just get on the road and go. Go anywhere and start all over.* I still had my credit cards with a $5,000 limit on each one of them. *I could just go to an ATM and withdraw as much as I could, and that would get us started. Momma and I could still go to New York or maybe Philly, get a cheap hotel. We both then could find jobs, and work until we could save up enough money so we could get our own place.*

And considering what happened, I didn't see why Momma wouldn't go for that. Besides, we would still need to get out of town.

I parked the car back at the Waffle House and walked down the hill to Keith's mansion. Once I approached the gate, I realized that if I put in the code, he might notice someone coming. I then thought about climbing the wall, but that only brought about the bad memories I had when I was in high school and all the boys laughed at me because I couldn't climb the rope in gym class.

"Okay, Ms. thang, man up," I said to myself.

I stood back and took a good look at the gate. It was about 12 feet high, but I thought if I could just jump up high enough to grip one of the railings, I could then walk up to the top, place my leg over to the other side of the gate, and jump down to the other side.

After twenty minutes or so of falling back down to the ground and scarring up my hands, on the fifteenth try, I did it. I made it over the wall to the other side.

I crept by the side of the house so as not to be noticed and then entered through the carport, which led into the kitchen. I suddenly heard voices yelling at one another as I entered the kitchen area.

"Bitch, you think you and your punk-ass son can just come in my house and take shit from me?" Keith yelled at Momma.

I lowered myself to the floor and crawled to the kitchen nook area, where I could look straight into the living room. I saw Momma standing in the middle of the room with tears in her eyes as Keith waved his gun at her, daring her not to move.

"Look, Cameron had nothing to do with this. It was my idea. So, please, just leave him out of this." Momma was crying and shaking like a leaf on a breezy day.

I looked about the room and noticed that Junior and Robin were sprawled out on the couch, knocked out. I didn't know whether they were dead or what.

"Bitch, if you don't tell me in five seconds where your punk-ass son and my money is, I'ma gonna blow off your muthafuckin' head, you understand me?" Keith placed his gun against the side of Momma's head.

I didn't know what to do. I looked around the kitchen to see what I could find to help defend Momma, but there wasn't anything I could use. I then noticed Momma's apron hanging off the side of the kitchen chair, and it appeared as if something was inside.

I crawled over to the chair and grabbed Momma's apron. Inside her apron pocket was a small handgun. Chile, I was so scared and nervous. When I took the gun in my hand, my hand started to shake like electricity was going through my entire body.

As I tried to calm myself, I heard, *BOOM! BOOM!*

I knew Keith had shot my Momma, so the tears had welled up inside of me, and the anger made my blood boil.

I closed my eyes and ran in the living room and started shooting. Once I had shot every bullet, I opened my eyes and saw Keith lying in front of me in his own pool of blood. I turned around, and there was Momma, lying there in her own blood, trying to catch her breath.

"Momma, you've been shot," I cried as I kneeled beside her and held her head in my lap.

"Yes, baby, it-it-it's o-o-okay," she whispered, choking on her on blood.

"Momma, you'll be all right. I'ma call nine one one." I pulled out my cell phone.

"No, baby, it-it-it will be fast-er if you go get the car and dri-dri-drive me t-t-to the hospital," she said, holding on to my arm.

"But, Momma, I parked the car all the way up where the Waffle House is, remember?"

"Yeah, baby, I-I-I remember. Just go now!" Momma sounded as though she was taking her last breath.

"Momma, I don't wanna leave you here like this," I said, tears streaming down my cheeks.

"Baby, st-sto-stop arguing wit-with me and get da-da car!" Momma stated squeezing my arm.

"Okay, Momma, I won't be long. I'ma run the whole way. Just hold on. Will you do that for me?" I stood up and wiped the tears from my face.

"Ye-ye-yes, ba-bab-baby, and Cam?"

"Yes, Momma."

"D-d-do me a fav-fav-favor?"

"Anything, Momma, anything."

"Turn, turn th-th-that light swi-swi-switch on by th-th-the side of da-da door."

"Light switch? Okay, Momma. Just hold on and I'll be back in five minutes, I promise."

I opened the front door and turned the light switch on and ran out as fast as I could. Once I got to the gate, I couldn't remember what the dayum code was, so I stood there trying my best to think.

Thank God, on the third attempt I finally got the gate open.

Just as I got to the bottom of the road, I suddenly heard an explosion that was so loud, it literally burned my eardrums. I turned around, and all I could see was Keith's mansion going up in flames. All I could do was fall to the ground as the tears poured down my face like a waterfall.

I then began to hear one of the neighbors's dog barking like crazy, and people began turning on their lights, trying to figure out where the loud explosion came from. I stood up and began walking as fast as I could up the road leading to the Waffle House, my heart beating a mile a minute. The more I wiped the tears away, the more they seemed to flow.

As I continued to walk, I saw fire trucks with sirens blaring coming down the road and heading towards Keith's mansion. All I wanted to do was get to my car. I only had about a block to go, but I felt my legs becoming wobbly as though they were about to give out, and my body was shaking as though I was freezing.

I heard my Momma's voice ringing in my ear. *"Come on, Cameron, man up."*

I made it to the car and locked myself in and cried and shook for several hours. I realized that when Momma had asked me to turn on the living room switch, she knew that it would blow up Keith's house.

I remembered Uncle Bill telling her before he left that all

she had to do was turn on the switch. Instead, I was the one to turn it on, as Momma had requested with her last breath. This time, I had lost her for good.  She wasn't coming back.

"What am I supposed to do now?" I tried to wipe my tears away. *"Man up,"* Again I heard Momma's voice ringing in my ears.

I sat there until dawn. *Where I could go?  Who could I call to comfort me?  Who will love and protect me now?* Momma had sacrificed her life for me, just to show me how much she truly loved me, but now I sat there feeling so alone. The love she had for me was now gone because she was gone.

As I sat and thought, there was only one person I could call on.  I took out my cell phone and made that call.

He answered on the first ring. "Hello."

"Can you come get me?" I asked, choking up.

"Who is this?"

"Cameron," I said in a whisper.

"Where are you?"

"I'm at the Waffle House on Route 10. You know where that is?"

"Yeah, I'm on my way."

# *C*hapter 24

Several months had passed since that night that I'd murdered Momma, my lover, former best friend, and Junior, the bastard that killed my brother Ray. Momma Gerdy thought it would be best if I sought some type of therapy after the tragic murders at the mansion. So, thanks to her, I was in therapy for a couple of months. My therapist said it would be cathartic, help my state of mind, if I wrote down my thoughts.

I knew I needed help because I had been crying practically every day till my eyes were bloodshot red and swollen to the point where I could hardly see out of them. Not to mention, the depression I felt every time I thought about that night, which seemed to consume me day and night.

The only two good things about seeing a therapist was, I'd begun to pray again, and my prescription drug, Valium. Chile boo, all I can say is, bless the doctor whoever invented Valium, because I had been floating on cloud nine for the past few weeks.

Anywho, let me catch y'all up on what's been going on since that night. The only person I could think of calling was Zack, and being the nice guy he was, he picked me up, and I'd been living with him ever since.

*Z* was a perfect gentleman. He took me in his home that night and held me while I cried myself to sleep. We still had not been intimate because he wanted me to make the first move. He wanted me to come to him when I thought I was ready.

To be honest, sex was the last thing on my mind. I loved *Z* for what he'd done by taking me in and being patient with me, but I wasn't in love with him. You know what I mean? Besides, I was still trying to deal with what I had done. Omaha's finest conducted an investigation about who planted the bombs in Keith's mansion. Momma Gerdy helped me with my alibi, telling the police I was at her house for dinner and stayed there for most of the evening. The police department had theorized that it was probably a rival gang that wanted to get back at Keith and Junior for trafficking on their turf.

The police had found my mother's body and wanted to know why she might have been there and whether or not I knew she would be there. I had informed them that I had reunited with her just a few months earlier and that we were working on our relationship as mother and son, but I didn't know she was coming to visit me that day. They also found Robin's body and wanted to know if I knew who she was. I told them she was my best friend and was dating Keith's brother, Junior.

They also wanted to know why I was living there and what was the relationship between Keith and me. What could I say but the truth? I informed them that Keith and I were lovers. They had disgust written all over their face, but I didn't care. I just wanted them to stop questioning me and go after some other gang members for what they did to three of the most important people in my life. I cried and carried on the whole time I was at the police station. Chile, I should have won an academy award for my performance.

*

The hardest part was attending my mother's funeral and then turning around the following day and attending Robin's funeral. *Z* was by my side the whole time for support, catering to my every need and want. He was absolutely fabulous about the whole ordeal.

Momma Gerdy and my Uncle Bill paid for both Momma's funeral and Robin's because Robin's momma, Auntie as I called her, was a total wreck. And she didn't have the funds to put her daughter away. Of course Momma Gerdy, had no idea where the money came from to pay for two funerals, but I knew as I watched Uncle Bill pull out his checkbook and paid the funeral director over twenty thousand dollars for both services.

The funeral director told me the day after they picked up my mother's body that her burns were severe, that she would have to have a closed casket at her funeral. So, as I sat there grieving her loss, I was hoping that maybe, just maybe, she had gotten out and wasn't in that coffin at all. I know that sounds absurd, but the thought of her not being in that coffin was making me feel better. Maybe I didn't kill her at all.

As I looked around the chapel in the funeral home, I realized that Momma didn't have a lot of friends. The only people there were Momma Gerdy, Uncle Bill, and Keisha, two or three people Momma knew around the way, me, Z, and the minister. I didn't know what the minister's sermon was about because, even though my body was there, my mind was somewhere else.

*

Later that night after Momma's burial and the small gathering at Momma Gerdy's house, Z and I left and went home. I'd taken a couple of Valiums that morning and found myself taking a couple more on the ride back home with him.

"Cameron," Z said in a whisper as he drove down the highway.

I was nodding off. "Yeah."

"I really would like to have a heart to heart talk with you," he stated in a low but serious tone.

"About?"

"I want to know the truth as to what happened that night." He looked at me out of the corner of his eyes.

"What do you mean?"

"The truth, babe. I wanna know the truth."

"I told you all I know, Z. I just can't handle this all by myself," I replied sniffling.

"Cam, you're not alone. I think you keep forgetting I'm an attorney, and I know, or shall I say, I feel you're keeping something from me."

Z was right. I never did tell him what happened. But how could I tell him the truth? And if I did tell him the truth, would he stop loving me and then ask me to leave?

"Babe, I know you're going through a lot. Regardless of what happened, I'm here for you, but I need you to trust me and be honest with me."

Z pulled up in front of his house and parked the car. I sat there trying to get my thoughts together, but I couldn't think straight because of the Valium.

"Come on, Cam, let's go in the house, get comfortable, and talk."

Z got out of the car and came over to the passenger side, opened the door, and helped me out of his car. We both were exhausted, and like all the other nights, he held me in his arms.

I began to tell him exactly what happened that night. Of course, I cried like a baby, but Z did not judge me. He held me tight until I couldn't cry anymore, and then he kissed me passionately.

I knew he had been waiting patiently for me to make the first move and because he had been there for me and now knew the truth of what had happened, he still loved me and wanted to be with me. And for that, I was eternally grateful, so I gave myself to him that night.

Unfortunately, it wasn't the toe-curling, mind-blowing sex that I loved, but this time around was different because, for once, I was satisfied that I had pleased someone other than myself. Chile, let me tell you, Z came three or four times, telling me how much he loved me and how much he wanted to take care of me. As much as I'd always wanted to hear those words from a man, I knew Z wasn't the one I wanted to spend my life with. He was a good man, a hard-working man, and an intelligent man as well, but I had love for him but wasn't *in* love with him.

As he lay beside me sleeping, I felt bad that I couldn't love him the way he loved me. I knew I would have to leave and start doing things for myself. Again, I kept hearing Momma's voice in the back of my head. *"Man up, baby, man up."*

Tomorrow was Robin's funeral, and I seriously didn't wanna go. How could I look down at her knowing I was responsible for her death? How could I console Auntie without feeling guilty? I was so restless lying in this bed, turning from one side to the other, I decided to turn the TV on and hoped that whatever was on could erase all of the thoughts creeping a mile a minute in and out my head.

I began flipping the channels, and oddly enough, there was a commercial on about joining the United States Army and "being all that you can be." At first I laughed at the thought of being in the Army. After all, who couldn't look at me and tell I wasn't gay? Anyhow, I continued to watch the commercial, which went on and on as though it was talking directly to me. Then I realized it was one of those infomercials. This brotha was talking about how he wanted to better his life for his family and in order to do that he had to become a man first, that being in the Army taught him how to be a man.

I started thinking about my life and the direction it was going in. I realized I wasn't doing a damn thing, other than sulking and having people take care of me. It was time for me to stop depending on other people and for me to "man up," as Momma would say, and take care of myself.

Besides, the military didn't look that hard, and it would give me the opportunity to travel, make my own money, and take care of myself.

After making the decision to join the Army, I felt like a big weight of some sort was lifted off my shoulders. I felt comforted and calm for some reason. I knew what I had to do. To-morrow morning I was going to the recruiting office and enlist in Uncle Sam's Army.

I began to drift off to sleep as I heard the announcer's voice on the infomercial say, *"Uncle Sam is looking for a few good men."*

I laughed to myself. *So am I.*

# $\mathcal{E}$pilogue

Well, chile, that's my story, and I'm sticking to it. Looking back, I really don't regret joining the military because it has done a lot for me. I've traveled, I've been able to take care of myself, I've met some really good people, and I even got married and had a son named after me. Unfortunately, my wife and I didn't work out. I guess she was looking for a man, a husband, and ultimately so was I.

I heard someone scream down the steps, "Camira, you gonna be going on in fifteen minutes."

Chile boo, anyways I still see my son from time to time. Although, I don't go around him dressed up like a woman.

Hell, Chauntel has never even seen me dressed up like a woman. I know, if she did, that bitch would gag, considering I look so much better than she does. Of course, I've only been doing drag for a short time. This performance I plan to do for Sean is only the second time I've actually performed in front of an audience. I honestly believe I was destined to do drag and perform in front of an audience. Even when I was a little boy, I used to dress up in my mother's clothes, stand in front of a mirror, and lip-synch to Patti Labelle's old jams.

It's funny because when I met my girl Akasha down at Bunn's one night, she thought she knew me and called me by some drag queen's name. I had to convince her that I wasn't her and that my name was Cameron. Well, honey, we became the best of friends, and before I knew it, Ms. Thang had me doing drag. I had become one of the dragons. Truth be told, it ain't like she had to twist my arm or hold a gun to my head, because I was all for it.

*

As for my family back in Omaha, I talk to Momma Gerdy at least every Sunday, just so she knows I'm still alive. She worries so. She's up in age now, but I love her just the same for all of what she has done for me and my sister Keshia.

As for my little sister Keisha, she's not so little anymore. She's married to an engineer and now lives in Charlotte, North Carolina with their one-year-old son. I'm so proud of her because with a husband, who ain't a bad-looking brotha by the way, and a one-year-old, she still finds time to go to school for her RN degree.

I still think of my real momma from time to time and wished she was still here. I miss her so much. But I think I'm gonna be okay. I know she's looking down from Heaven and telling me to "man up," but that's just not who I am. I am what I am, and I have gone through a lot in my lifetime to be who I am, and I make no apologies for it. People have to accept me, or they can kick rocks, as Keisha would say.

I'm still in the United States Army, and thank God for our President Barack Obama, who initiated the repeal on gays in the military, I still have a job. The morning I signed up for the Army, I was lucky enough to be able to leave that day. I never said anything to Z about going because I was afraid he would try to talk me out of it.

After I joined, I did send him a Dear John and explained to him why I had to leave. He said he was broken-hearted, but he understood that a man had to do what a man had to do. Even me. Of course, he thought that comment was funny, I didn't.

Anyways, we've kept in contact over the years, and he had actually met someone and fell deeply in love, and they have been together for the past couple of years. I would be lying if I said I wasn't a wee bit jealous, but I am happy for him and his new partner.

Oh by the way, I actually got a letter from him a couple days ago, and he had the nerve to invite me to him and his lover's anniversary party. Chile boo, I'm happy for him, but I ain't that happy, you know. When my father/uncle died a few years ago, I went home for the funeral. I did stop by and pay *Z* a visit. At the time he was still single, so we hooked up, and yes, I let him hit it for old times' sake. And, again, it wasn't all that, but *Z* was happy and still talking about how he was still in love with me, blah blah blah.

I have met a lot of new people over the years, some good, and some bad, but ultimately, life is good. Now, when I met Sean Mathews, I thought he would be the one. The one that I prayed to God for every night.

I would get on my knees and say to God, "Just Make Him Beautiful." I met Sean in Basic Training. I didn't speak to him at the time because I really didn't know what to say. I knew he wasn't gay, just by the way he carried himself, but I was going to do everything in my power to get at him.

Once we graduated from Basic Training, I found out where he was going to be stationed and I had a friend of mine in the administration department change my orders so I go to Fort Meade, Maryland as well.

Sean Mathews, what can I say about Sean? I first have to admit that I wasn't honest with him about a lot of things. I'd never told him about my relationship with my brother, or the relationship I had with Keith. I never told him about my mother being in an institution or that I had killed the three most important people in my life.

As feminine as I am, I wanted Sean to accept me as a friend. I needed Sean in my life because he to me was the epitome of what a man was supposed to be. He carried himself in such a way that I loved him the first day I laid eyes on him.

Chile, I shall not forget. We were still in Basic Training and had just finished PT. We were standing outside the mess hall in line for breakfast, and he was standing right in front of me, sweat pouring of him like a waterfall. He had his OD-green gym shorts on and had taken off his T-shirt. Even his back had muscles.

Lawd, I stared at him from the top of his six-two frame to his ankles and felt my nature rise, as well as the moisture from within my thighs. Now, that was the first time I had experienced both of my sex organs becoming excited at the same time. I wanted to somehow get in front of him just to see what this black Arnold Schwarzenegger brotha looked like.

But there was nothing I could do because, as a new recruit, you're not allowed to say shit while standing in line, and if you do, you will be severely reprimanded. So, I waited until we got inside the mess hall, where I could possibly bump into him, and that way, I would get a better look.We made it into the mess hall, and Sean sat with, I assume, his friends from his squad. I, on the other hand, sat with those in my squad. I wasn't friends with any of them, but I had a direct view of Private Sean Mathews. I noticed that Sean had finished his breakfast and got up to dump his tray in the trash.

Needless to say I got up, and as I was about to dump my food in the trash as well, I deliberately bumped into him, and he turned around.

"I'm sorry. My bad," I said nervously.

"No problem, shawty." He smiled at me, showing his dimples.

Chile, I almost fainted. I looked up at him with his mocha-colored complexion and chiseled chest. I felt like I had died and gone to Heaven. I stood there frozen and watched as he placed his scraps in the trash, and his plates and silverware in the sink. I couldn't take my eyes off of him because as I looked across his chiseled chest and at his succulent man nipples, my eyes scrolled farther down and I swear to God, this brotha wore no underwear because I could clearly see the print of his half-erect penis protruding from his shorts. Honey, that shit looked so good, my mouth began to water. I became so flustered, I was afraid I would instinctively reach out and grab it. I dumped my whole tray in the trash bin and ran out of there.

It seems like it was only yesterday, but it's been almost four years since that happened. Sean and I did become the best of friends and even fell in love with each other. However, we seemed to have fallen in love with each other at separate times.

That day I fell in love with Sean, he was already in love and married and had a child to boot. Unfortunately, when he finally realized he was in love with me, we were standing in church at the altar. I was the groom, and he was my best man.

When Sean burst out and said that he loved me and didn't want me to make the same mistake he did, I was stunned like a deer caught in headlights. But it was the wrong time. I married Chauntel anyway. I'm not sure what would have happened if Sean hadn't been picked up by the MPs that day, but I guess we will never know.

*

"Camira, you're on in one minute, girl! You betta hurry up!" I heard Akasha yelling down the stairs at me.

I yelled back, "Okay already."

Well, honies, as they say, the show must go on. You know, I was going to lip-synch Vanessa Bell Armstrong's "Congratulations," but so much had changed between Sean and me that to show him I still care in my own way and that I can still laugh about what we had, I changed the song to Beyonce's "Single Ladies." Hopefully, he will get the irony of that. It's funny, I joined the military hoping it would make me more of a man, when in fact, it seemed to do the complete opposite, chile boo. Anyway, as I was about to get up, I took a real hard look at myself in the mirror and I realized how beautiful I was as a woman, and then it finally hit me. I had an epiphany. All the years I had been praying to God to "Just Make Him Beautiful," I realized He already had.

# Also By Mike Warren

## PART 1

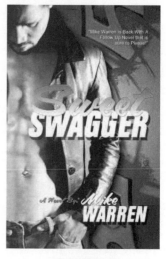

## PART 2

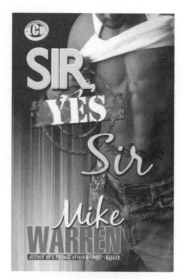

## PART 3

# CHECK OUT THESE LCB SEQUELS

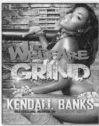

**MAIL TO:**
PO Box 423
Brandywine, MD 20613
301-362-6508

# ORDER FORM

| Ship to: | |
|---|---|
| Address: | |

| Date: | | Phone: | |
|---|---|---|---|
| Email: | | | |
| | City & State: | | Zip: |

Make all money orders and cashiers checks payable to:  Life Changing Books

| Qty. | ISBN | Title | Release Date | Price |
|---|---|---|---|---|
| | 0-9741394-2-4 | Bruised by Azarel | Jul-05 | $ 15.00 |
| | 0-9741394-7-5 | Bruised 2: The Ultimate Revenge by Azarel | Oct-06 | $ 15.00 |
| | 0-9741394-3-2 | Secrets of a Housewife by J. Tremble | Feb-06 | $ 15.00 |
| | 0-9741394-6-7 | The Millionaire Mistress by Tiphani | Nov-06 | $ 15.00 |
| | 1-934230-99-5 | More Secrets More Lies by J. Tremble | Feb-07 | $ 15.00 |
| | 1-934230-95-2 | A Private Affair by Mike Warren | May-07 | $ 15.00 |
| | 1-934230-96-0 | Flexin & Sexin Volume 1 | Jun-07 | $ 15.00 |
| | 1-934230-89-8 | Still a Mistress by Tiphani | Nov-07 | $ 15.00 |
| | 1-934230-91-X | Daddy's House by Azarel | Nov-07 | $ 15.00 |
| | 1-934230-88-X | Naughty Little Angel by J. Tremble | Feb-08 | $ 15.00 |
| | 1-934230820 | Rich Girls by Kendall Banks | Oct-08 | $ 15.00 |
| | 1-934230839 | Expensive Taste by Tiphani | Nov-08 | $ 15.00 |
| | 1-934230782 | Brooklyn Brothel by C. Stecko | Jan-09 | $ 15.00 |
| | 1-934230669 | Good Girl Gone bad by Danette Majette | Mar-09 | $ 15.00 |
| | 1-934230804 | From Hood to Hollywood by Sasha Raye | Mar-09 | $ 15.00 |
| | 1-934230707 | Sweet Swagger by Mike Warren | Jun-09 | $ 15.00 |
| | 1-934230677 | Carbon Copy by Azarel | Jul-09 | $ 15.00 |
| | 1-934230723 | Millionaire Mistress 3 by Tiphani | Nov-09 | $ 15.00 |
| | 1-934230715 | A Woman Scorned by Ericka Williams | Nov-09 | $ 15.00 |
| | 1-934230685 | My Man Her Son by J. Tremble | Feb-10 | $ 15.00 |
| | 1-924230731 | Love Heist by Jackie D. | Mar-10 | $ 15.00 |
| | 1-934230812 | Flexin & Sexin Volume 2 | Apr-10 | $ 15.00 |
| | 1-934230748 | The Dirty Divorce by Miss KP | May-10 | $ 15.00 |
| | 1-934230758 | Chedda Boyz by CJ Hudson | Jul-10 | $ 15.00 |
| | 1-934230766 | Snitch by VegasClarke | Oct-10 | $ 15.00 |
| | 1-934230693 | Money Maker by Tonya Ridley | Oct-10 | $ 15.00 |
| | 1-934230774 | The Dirty Divorce Part 2 by Miss KP | Nov-10 | $ 15.00 |
| | 1-934230170 | The Available Wife by Carla Pennington | Jan-11 | $ 15.00 |
| | 1-934230774 | One Night Stand by Kendall Banks | Feb-11 | $ 15.00 |
| | 1-934230278 | Bitter by Danette Majette | Feb-11 | $ 15.00 |
| | 1-934230299 | Married to a Balla by Jackie D. | May-11 | $ 15.00 |
| | 1-934230308 | The Dirty Divorce Part 3 by Miss KP | Jun-11 | $ 15.00 |
| | 1-934230316 | Next Door Nympho By CJ Hudson | Jun-11 | $ 15.00 |
| | 1-934230286 | Bedroom Gangsta by J. Tremble | Sep-11 | $ 15.00 |
| | 1-934230340 | Another One Night Stand by Kendall Banks | Oct-11 | $ 15.00 |
| | 1-934230359 | The Available Wife  Part 2 by Carla Pennington | Nov-11 | $ 15.00 |
| | 1-934230332 | Wealthy & Wicked by Chris Renee | Jan-12 | $ 15.00 |
| | 1-934230375 | Life After a Balla by Jackie D. | Mar-12 | $ 15.00 |
| | 1-934230251 | V.I.P. by Azarel | Apr-12 | $ 15.00 |
| | 1-934230383 | Welfare Grind by Kendall Banks | May-12 | $ 15.00 |
| | 1-934230413 | Still Grindin' by Kendall Banks | Sep-12 | $ 15.00 |
| | 1-934230391 | Paparazzi by Miss KP | Oct-12 | $ 15.00 |
| | | | Total for Books | $ |

| | |
|---|---|
| * Prison Orders- Please allow up to three (3) weeks for delivery. | Shipping Charges (add $4.95 for 1-4 books*) $ |
| | Total Enclosed (add lines) $ |

Please Note: We are not held responsible for returned prison orders. Make sure the facility will receive books before ordering.

*Shipping and Handling of 5-10 books is $6.95, please contact us if your order is more than 10 books.
(301)362-6508